Wish Upon a Sleepover

SUZANNE SELFORS

[Imprint]
MAKE YOUR MARK

New York

SQUARE FISH

An imprint of Macmillan Publishing Group, LLC
175 Fifth Avenue, New York, NY 10010
mackids.com

Square Fish and the Square Fish logo are trademarks of Macmillan and
are used by Imprint under license from Macmillan.

Our books may be purchased in bulk for promotional, educational, or business use. Please
contact your local bookseller or the Macmillan Corporate and Premium Sales Department at
(800) 221-7945 ext. 5442 or by email at MacmillanSpecialMarkets@macmillan.com.

Library of Congress Cataloging-in-Publication Data
Names: Selfors, Suzanne, author.
Title: Wish upon a sleepover / Suzanne Selfors.
Description: New York : Imprint, 2018. | Summary: A group of
misfits has a sleepover that involves a scavenger hunt and slightly
magical soup in this story of newfound friendship in unexpected places.
Identifiers: LCCN 2016035864 (print) | LCCN 2017011051 (ebook) |
ISBN 978-1-250-30874-0 (paperback) | ISBN 978-1-250-10973-6 (ebook)
Subjects: | CYAC: Friendship—Fiction. | Sleepovers—Fiction. | Treasure hunt
(Game)—Fiction.
Classification: LCC PZ7.S456922 (ebook) | LCC PZ7.S456922 Sl 2017 (print) |
DDC [Fic]—dc23
LC record available at https://lccn.loc.gov/2016035864

[Imprint]
MAKE YOUR MARK

@ImprintReads
Originally published in the United States by Imprint
First Square Fish edition, 2019
Book designed by Heather Palisi
Illustrations courtesy of Alia Ching and Mio Buono/Shutterstock
Imprint logo designed by Amanda Spielman
Square Fish logo designed by Filomena Tuosto

1   3   5   7   9   10   8   6   4   2

Lexile: 600L

Steal time, steal looks, but never ever steal books.

For my mom, Marilyn, who helped
me plan the best sleepover ever: pajamas,
waffles at noon, and a trail of riddles that
led to buried treasure. Thanks, Mom!

TO Caterin
From Cookie

Happy BirthDAY!
We Sould have
a sleepover!

Dear Reader,

There is a famous story about people working together to take something quite humble and turn it into something quite extraordinary. Best known as "Stone Soup," the story has traveled the globe, from the terraced mountains of China, through the bustling cities of Northern Europe, to the sun-dappled islands of the Pacific. Across continents and oceans, the story has flown, and wherever it touches down, that culture makes it their own.

But this *particular* version has never been told until now.

Contents

The Boy Who Is So Very Rude

I don't like the boy on the third floor.

Actually, I hate him.

I know *hate* is an ugly word, and I tried really hard not to feel that way, but sometimes feelings can't be helped. Last week, Tutu told me that bad feelings are like pimples, and when they pop up, you can squeeze out the toxins, or you can cover them and pretend they don't exist.

"Are those my only choices?" I asked.

She nodded in her very wise Tutu way.

"Just stay away from him," Mom said.

"But there's only one elevator, and that's where I keep seeing him."

"Then take the stairs."

"Why should *I* take the stairs? I've lived here longer." It was a matter of seniority. Plus, walking up six flights was not something I wanted to add to my daily routine. I was already incredibly busy spying on the Haileys.

There are six Haileys at my school. Hailey, spelled with an *I*. Haighley, spelled with a *GH*. Hayley, spelled with a *Y*. Heyley, spelled with an *EY*. Heeyley, spelled with three *E*'s. And the most confusing of all, Heighleigh, spelled with two *E*'s, two *I*'s, and two *GH*'s.

My name is Leilani. It's a Hawaiian name that means "heavenly flowers." Tutu's real name is also Leilani, but we call her Tutu because it means "grandparent" in Hawaiian. She's actually my great-grandmother, but she doesn't like being reminded of that fact because it makes her feel old. Tutu's from Hawaii, but now she lives with us in Seattle. She grew up on Kauai, the garden island. I visited Kauai when I was a baby, but I don't remember the trip. Mom and I haven't been back since my dad died. I was a baby then, too.

Tutu and Mom are full Hawaiian, but I'm hapa haole, which means "part." My mom and my dad both grew up in Seattle, and that was where they met. Mom's name is Alani, which means "orange tree." My dad's name was Conrad, which is an old Germanic name that means "bold." I know the definitions of everyone's name because I bought a book of names from the dollar bin at the public library. I looked up each different spelling for *Hailey*, and no matter how you spell it, it always means the same thing—"a hayfield."

The reason I spy on the Haileys is because I want to join their group. It's my goal for sixth grade. It won't be an easy feat. The Haileys are like an exclusive club that you have to be invited to join. They're super popular, and even though I haven't spoken much to any of them, they all seem nice. And they're always having fun. At some point in first grade, their names brought them together, and they've been inseparable best friends ever since. If I lived in Hawaii, there'd probably be more Leilanis at my school, and maybe we'd all be friends. That would be great.

At lunch, the Haileys sit at the big round table and swap food. At break they hang out in the concrete tunnel and share secrets. And after school, they wave goodbye and blow kisses and promise to call one another if anything exciting happens on the ride home.

The most exciting thing that happened to me on my ride home was when my bus driver got an attack of acid reflux and had to pull over. We thought she was going to barf, but all she did was burp super loud a whole bunch of times. I tried using acid reflux as an excuse not to go to school the next day, but my mom knew I was faking. She's a nurse, so it's nearly impossible to fool her.

I considered changing my name, as a way to infiltrate their group. Maybe I could spell it *Hey! Lee!* I thought that was funny. But I knew the change would upset Tutu. Besides, as soon as the Haileys get to know me, they'll want me in their group, regardless of my name. I'm sure of this. I just need the perfect moment to get their attention. The more information I gather, the better my chances of creating that perfect moment. And then we'll all be friends.

But that boy from the third floor—I no longer care about being his friend. When he moved in last month, I thought, *Great, a new kid in the building.* I tried to be nice to him, three times in a row, but he ignored me. The first time went like this—he was already in the elevator when I ran into the lobby. I'd just gotten off the school bus and I was starving. "Hey, hold the doors, will ya?" I called. But the elevator started to close and the boy just stood there, staring at his shoes. I shoved my hand inside and practically got it cut off. "Why didn't you hold the doors?" I asked as I squeezed in. I pushed button number six.

He didn't say anything, just kept staring at his shoes. They weren't sneakers, like most kids wear. They were brown leather and scuffed. His hair was so blond I could see right through to his scalp. And his face was so pale I could see a blue vein at his temple.

My backpack bumped against the side of the elevator as I tried to find a comfortable place to stand. It was pretty crowded in there because the boy had a huge leather suitcase that was covered in stickers of places like London, Paris, and New York City. He also had a plastic pet carrier. "You moving in?" I asked.

He didn't say anything.

I reached into my pocket and pulled out a pack of gum. "Want a piece?"

Without even saying *no thank you*, he turned his back to me. *What* was his problem? Maybe he was shy. Shy people need a little extra understanding. I know because my best friend's so shy that sometimes, if she gets really nervous, she pees her pants a little. But she really doesn't want me telling anyone that. "So, my name's Leilani. I live on the sixth floor. What's your name?"

He didn't answer, just kept ignoring me. I decided to try again.

"What's in there? Is it a cat?" I tapped on the top of the carrier and heard a soft meow.

The boy slid the carrier behind his suitcase so I couldn't reach it.

Maybe the cat was shy, too. You never know.

"Where do you go to school? Where'd you live before you moved here? Have you been to all those places on the stickers? How old are you? I can show you around if you want."

The elevator stopped on the third floor and the doors opened. The boy grabbed the handle of his suitcase and the handle of his cat carrier and darted out.

"Let me know if you want a tour of the neighborhood," I said.

He didn't look back.

Weird, I thought.

The second time we rode the elevator together, I tried to make polite conversation, because that's what a nice person does, but again he said nothing.

The third time, when he got off on the third floor, I decided he wasn't shy, because even a shy person can say one simple word, like *bye*.

"Never mind," I told him, but he was already heading down the hallway with his cat carrier. "I don't have time to give you a tour. I'm way too busy." I pressed the sixth-floor button again.

But just as the elevator doors shut, I heard him whisper, as if he were talking to a teeny, tiny mouse, "My name is William."

Autumn, Not Fall

Mom, Tutu, and I live in apartment 6B, on the top floor of our building. There's nothing special about our building. It's made of bricks, and the lobby floor is cruddy old chipped tile. A plastic plant sits in the corner of the lobby, near the mailboxes. The manager, Ms. Grutch, thinks real plants are too much of a bother. The fake plant is covered in dust and spiderwebs. Recently, someone started tossing cigarette butts into its green pot. It's real sad-looking. One time, Tutu shoved it into the garbage can. "Put it out of its misery," she said. But someone fished it out.

The building across the street is only a few years old, and it has condos instead of apartments. The doorman wears a gray uniform, and he holds the door open when the owners have groceries. That's where Hailey spelled with an *I* lives. She doesn't ride my bus because she gets picked up after school. I can see right into her apartment when I look out my living room and bedroom windows.

Mom says I shouldn't look into other people's apartments. But Tutu does it all the time. She knows when the old Croatian ladies are playing bridge, and when the man with the white beard gets a new stack of books from the library. And I know when Hailey Chun is having another one of her sleepovers.

The Haileys have sleepovers every weekend. And they only invite each other. Heeyley with three *E*'s had a cupcake sleepover. She brought little cupcake-shaped invitations and handed them out at the big round table during lunch. The plan was to bake and decorate cupcakes and then eat them while watching movies. It sounded super fun. Who doesn't love cupcakes?

Haighley with a *GH* had a beauty sleepover. They brought makeup and nail polish and gave each other makeovers. And Hayley with a *Y* had a dance party sleepover. They made up dances to their favorite songs.

I always eat lunch next to the big round table on purpose so I can hear all about these parties. And I've watched a few from my bedroom window.

"They're planning another sleepover," I report to Autumn.

Autumn Maxwell has been my best friend since kindergarten, when we met in the principal's office. I was there because I'd kicked Jeremy Bishop in the shins, and she was there because she'd peed her pants a little. If you kick someone in the shins at school, even if that someone was pulling your hair, you get a lecture from the principal and you get sent home with a note that has to be signed and returned. If you pee your pants at school, they make you choose a clean pair from a bin that is kept in the nurse's office. The bin's full of old, ugly sweatpants that no one wants to wear—that's why they ended up in the bin. So Autumn had to spend the rest of the day in a hideous pair of orange sweats that went all the way up to her armpits, and I had to spend the day worrying if my mom was going to take away my TV privileges.

She did. I didn't get to watch the Disney Channel for a whole week.

"I'm in Mr. Wren's class," I told Autumn.

"I'm in Ms. Pearl's class," she told me. She scratched her nose. Autumn has the kind of skin that is super pale and covered in freckles, like a connect-the-dots picture. When we were in second grade, I did try to connect them, with an ink pen, and it took three whole days for the lines to wash off. I felt really bad, so I drew on my face, too, so we'd match.

"Why'd you pee your pants?"

"I felt anxious."

"What's that mean?" I'm pretty sure Autumn was the only kid in kindergarten who used that word.

"It means 'nervous.'"

"How come you felt nervous?"

"Because I don't like Sharing Time."

Wow, how could a person not like Sharing Time? You got to stand in front of the class and tell them something amazing about yourself or your family. I loved it! That very day I'd brought a can of macadamia nuts, one for everyone in class. But there was this kid whose head would blow up like a balloon if he ate a nut, so I had to promise I wouldn't open the can. I told the class how macadamia nut trees were brought to Hawaii over a hundred years ago to plant around sugarcane fields, to protect the cane from strong winds. And then I told them that if you ate too many macadamia nuts, you'd get diarrhea. I'd learned that the hard way.

Autumn and I waited in the principal's office forever. Then the principal handed me my note. "Be sure your mom signs this," she told me. "And no more kicking." Then she handed Autumn a clear ziplock plastic bag. "Don't forget these." Autumn's pee-soaked jeans were sealed inside. "Take this back to your classroom."

Autumn held the bag between her thumb and pointer finger. "Are you trying to humiliate me?" she asked the principal.

I didn't know what that meant, but I instantly knew this girl was different. I grabbed the bag and stuck it into my backpack so no one would see it as we walked down the hall.

From that moment on, we were best friends. After school, we'd hang out at my house. And on weekends, we'd go to the community center pool. Even though Autumn couldn't swim, she'd still go with me. While I did the lazy river and the slide, she'd sit on the steps in the shallow end and read whatever magazine she'd found in the lobby. We did everything together, and we still do. Except for spying on the Haileys. That's my thing.

"Yep, it's another sleepover," I confirm. It's lunchtime and we are in our usual seats near the big round table.

"While I'm no fan of the Haileys, I appreciate their predictability," Autumn says. She pulls the lid off a Tupperware container. It has separate compartments. Her sandwich fits in the sandwich spot. Her orange is sliced to fit into the fruit spot. And her juice box fits perfectly into the juice box spot. She eats the same thing every day. Monday or Friday, Tuesday, Thursday, or Wednesday, Autumn has apple juice, orange slices, and a crustless cheese sandwich with iceberg lettuce and no mayo. It's the kind of fake cheese that if you roll it up into a ball, it bounces. Autumn always saves a special treat for the very end—a chocolate-covered macadamia nut. Tutu introduced them to her when we first became friends, and she's loved them ever since. And eating only one a day won't give you diarrhea.

"It's a barbecue sleepover," I tell her. I rub my neck. Sometimes it gets stiff because I have to lean my head to the right so I can hear the Haileys better. "I love barbecue."

"I'll never understand the allure of sauce-drenched meat." Autumn carefully lifts her sandwich from the box. She doesn't like it when one piece of food touches another piece of food. I'd already pointed out that the sandwich, oranges, apple juice, and chocolate-covered macadamia nut all end up touching in her stomach, so what did it matter?

"Everything matters," she'd said.

Autumn is named after autumn, the season, because that's when she was born. Maybe her parents figured that *Fall* wouldn't make a very good name. I think they should have named her after someone smart, like Einstein. Autumn is the smartest kid at our school, only she's too shy to let anyone know.

I lean sideways. "Oooh, Heighleigh's dad is going to get the food from Voodoo Barbecue. That's the best. Especially the shredded pork." I lean some more. That's when Hailey Chun stops talking, turns, and glares at me.

"What's your problem?" she asks.

"Uh, oh, hi, Hailey." I open my yogurt and stir the peaches up from the bottom of the container, acting like I haven't been listening. Acting like I don't care.

But I do care.

Having only one friend used to be fine with me. Autumn and I get along perfectly. And we're almost always together. But her parents got divorced last summer, so now Autumn spends every other weekend at her dad's new house, way up in Bellingham. Which means that when she's gone, I don't have anyone to hang out with except for Mom and Tutu. Mom is usually busy working the weekend shift, and if Tutu isn't watching TV, or napping, or complaining about the lack of sunshine, the only other thing she wants to do is walk to the corner market for snacks. Once, I convinced her to go to the community pool, but she refused to get into the water. "It's too cold!" she complained. "And the chlorine makes my eyes burn!" She grew up swimming in the Pacific Ocean, where the water is so blue and so warm she even swam in the rain. So while Tutu sat in the lobby, in her plastic swim cap and pink bathrobe, telling everyone that they should move to Hawaii because there's no chlorine in the water, I realized that having only one friend wasn't the best situation to be in.

Well, it's going to change this year. The Haileys have a party every weekend, and they don't know this yet, but soon they'll start including me. I just have to figure out how to get onto their radar.

They huddle closer together and lower their voices. With all the racket in the rest of the cafeteria, I can't hear them any longer. So I eat my yogurt. Autumn takes tiny bites of her sandwich, working her way around the edges. She chews with her front teeth, like a squirrel. She has big, round squirrel eyes, too. My mom always says that Autumn is as cute as a button.

"There's this new exhibit at the science center about the human brain, and I was thinking we could go," she says.

"Yeah . . . maybe," I mumble. Then I put down my yogurt container. "Hey! What if I have a sleepover?" The idea sends a shiver up my spine.

Autumn lowers her sandwich.

"That's what I'll do! I'll have one and invite the Haileys, and then they'll see that I'm super fun and they'll start inviting me to their parties." Somebody shine a spotlight on my head, because my idea is brilliant!

"A party?" Autumn's eyes get even bigger. One of her curls falls across her forehead.

"My sleepover will be great. You'll see." I pause. "No, wait, forget that. It won't be *great*. It'll be the *best sleepover in the history of the world*! And you'll be there, too."

"Me?" Autumn drops her half-eaten sandwich onto her napkin. "I gotta go to the bathroom." And off she scurries.

I glance over at the Haileys. They're looking at photos on Heeyley Kerrigan's phone and laughing. One day I'll be laughing with them. But right now, I have a party to plan.

Prepare to be amazed.

Tutu On Board

"Mom, can I have a sleepover?"

"Autumn is always welcome here. You know that." Mom is in her bedroom, putting on her blue scrubs. I'm sitting on the edge of her bed.

"I want to invite six kids from my school *and* Autumn."

"Oh." She reaches into the closet and grabs a cardigan. "Seven kids? When would you have this sleepover?"

"Not this weekend, because the Haileys are already having a party, and Autumn will be at her dad's. So mine would be the next weekend. Saturday night."

"Well, I'm glad you want to have friends over, but I won't be off my shift until four AM. And"—she lowers her voice—"that's a lot of kids. You know how tired Tutu gets. I don't think she can handle it." She walks into the hallway.

I slide off the bed and hurry after her. "Tutu doesn't have to do anything."

"I don't know. . . ." She steps into the kitchen. "Where would your guests sleep?"

"In the living room, in sleeping bags," I say. Mom frowns as she puts on her cardigan. We both look over the kitchen counter, into the living room, where Tutu is watching TV in her pink bathrobe, like she always does after dinner. "I'll ask her," I say.

Tutu is eighty-three years old. She used to work at a travel agency, but her customer-service attitude got bad, and she started getting things mixed up, like sending a honeymoon couple to Tijuana instead of Tahiti. And then she had a heart attack and she couldn't live alone anymore, so that's when she came to Seattle to live with us. She spends so much time on our couch that the cushion on one end has a permanent dent in it, shaped just like her butt.

"Tutu?" I say as I sit next to her. She smells like coconut lotion, which she always rubs on her elbows and knees.

"Clicker." She holds out her hand. "I don't like the

news. Too much hatred in the world." I hand the clicker to her, and she changes the channel to a talk show. "Why can't people get along? When I was a little girl in the camp, no one robbed anyone. We all went fishing and shared our catch."

Tutu always calls the place where she grew up a camp. It was owned by the Lihue Plantation. Her dad worked for the sugar company, cutting sugarcane, and her mom raised eight children in a tiny two-bedroom cottage that didn't have a bathroom. All the families in the camp had to share an outhouse and a washroom. Tutu loves telling stories about her childhood, like how her grandfather used to hunt wild pigs with a bow and arrow, and how she and her brothers would use nets to trap black river crabs. And how she once saw a menehune, which is a tiny little person who lives in the forest. Mom says that some of the stories are true, and some are products of Tutu's very active imagination.

Usually I like listening to Tutu's stories, but right now I want to talk about my party.

"Fishing sounds nice, Tutu." I pause. "Um, can I have six friends over for a sleepover, plus Autumn, on the weekend after this weekend? Mom won't be here because she's got the night shift."

"I'm not cooking," she says, changing to a weather

report. The reporter says it might get cold enough to snow. Snow would definitely put Tutu in a grumpier-than-usual mood.

"You don't have to cook. We can feed ourselves."

"I'm not cleaning."

"You don't have to clean. I'll do it." I smile. This is looking promising.

"Tutu, don't let Leilani pressure you," Mom calls from the kitchen. "Seven is a lot of kids. You'll get tired."

"I'm always tired," Tutu complains. "When I was young, I never got tired, even after working at the factory all day. I could label pineapple cans faster than anyone. And when I got home, I still had enough strength to do my chores and homework." She changes to a game show called *Hollywood Squares*.

I don't want Tutu to get distracted by the show, so I lean real close. "What do you think about the sleepover?" I ask.

"I'm not reading bedtime stories, or wiping noses, or driving kids home if they get scared."

"You don't have to do any of that stuff." Does she think we're five years old? Besides, she doesn't have a driver's license anymore. "So it's okay? I can have the sleepover?"

She grunts.

I throw my arms around her and kiss her wrinkled cheek. "You're the best tutu ever."

"This is true," she says.

"*Aloha au iā ʻoe*," I tell her. That means "I love you" in Hawaiian.

"*Aloha au iā ʻoe*," she says back.

The Planning Committee

I need a theme for my sleepover. It has to be something the Haileys haven't done. It has to be amazing, so that my sleepover will go down in history, and I'll get a reputation as an extraordinary party planner. Then the Haileys will ask me to organize all future parties. And that will seal our friendship. And I will no longer have to spend every other weekend with just Tutu and Mom, doing errands like getting Tutu's prescriptions filled or shopping for seaweed crackers and prune juice.

I decide to call a special meeting with my planning committee.

"So what do you think? Maybe a circus theme? Or is that too babyish?"

"Why are we exposing ourselves to potential frostbite?" Autumn asks.

"Because I don't want anyone eavesdropping and copying my ideas," I tell her. Even though it's a really cold day for Seattle and we are still expecting snow, I've chosen a bench outside the school's office building for our meeting. "Oh, I know. How about a supermodel theme?"

Autumn wraps her scarf around her neck. Her teeth chatter as she clutches her Tupperware box. "I have no opinion regarding the theme."

"But I need your help." I nudge her with my elbow. "Come on. It's gonna be fun!" She stares at me with her big eyes. If I have to say one negative thing about Autumn, it's this—she can be a real drag when it comes to parties. She never wants to go, and if she does go, she always sits in the corner with a book. "Everyone can dress up and we can do a runway show. What else says 'supermodel'?"

"An eating disorder," Autumn mumbles.

"Huh?" I frown. "How come you're so grumpy?"

"Because my fingers are too frozen to open my lunch, and I'm famished. You know I get low blood sugar." The tip of her nose has turned red. My fingers are okay, so I open the container for her.

Last month, the Haileys got matching lunch bags. They're earth-friendly bags that can be washed and reused. Not only are the Haileys best friends who coordinate their lunches, but they also care about the environment. I thought it would be cool if Autumn and I got matching bags, so I mentioned it. "I'm not going to put my food in *a bag*," Autumn said. "Cross-contamination might occur." She's very serious about the not-touching thing.

"Hey, cuz!" a voice calls.

I groan and try to hide under my hood, but it's too late. Todd Burl walks up to us.

"Hey, why are you sitting outside?" he asks. "It's, like, thirty degrees out here."

I fold my arms and glare at him. "We're busy, Todd. Go away."

Maybe it sounds like I'm being mean, but Todd Burl drives me crazy. He's loud and obnoxious, and always interrupts. He likes to tell everyone that we're cousins. Actually, my dad and his mom were cousins, which makes Todd and me *second* cousins, and that means we're barely related. He's the tallest kid in sixth grade. Compared to everyone else, he looks like he's on stilts. And he's super skinny because he grew so fast last summer. Everybody knows Todd because he's a star basketball player. And also because he can fart on command. Mom told me he's lactose intolerant and that's why he's so gassy. His basketball friends think his farting is hilarious, but I think it's a form of domestic terrorism. 'Cause what can you do? You have to breathe, right?

Todd's name comes from the Old English word *todde*, which means "fox." A long time ago, it was a nickname given to people who were clever or had red hair, like a fox. Todd doesn't have red hair, and he doesn't seem any smarter than anyone else. Especially not Autumn.

"That sandwich looks good," he tells Autumn. The florescent orange glows between the slices of bread. "Is it cheese?"

"Uh-huh," she says, her cheeks turning as red as her nose. She doesn't like Todd, either.

"Are you gonna eat it? 'Cause I'll eat it if you're not hungry."

"You're not supposed to eat cheese, Todd," I remind him. "Now, go away. We have stuff to talk about." If he hears us talking about my sleepover, he'll tell everyone. I want to keep it a secret until I figure out the theme.

"Say it," he says with a wicked smile. "Say I'm your cousin."

"No way."

"Say it or I'll let one fly. I just had a milk shake, and it's churning up real good."

Autumn starts squirming. She pulls her scarf up around her nose.

"I won't and you can't make me." I don't care if he ate an entire cow, I will never say it. Never!

He squeezes his eyes shut. The fart makes a squeaking sound and takes a real long time coming out. "You're disgusting," I tell him.

He snickers. "One of these days, Leilani, you'll admit we're cousins." Then he walks into the school.

"Never!" I yell. Even with the wind blowing, it takes a few minutes for the stench to go away. "Gross. How are we supposed to eat after that?"

Autumn and I stare at our food. I imagine Todd's fart germs clinging to my sandwich. Is that possible? I'm about to ask Autumn if a fart makes germs when something catches my attention. The building across from us has a long bay of windows. The Haileys are walking past the windows, carrying their matching lunch bags to their lockers. Whenever they walk, they huddle real close, like one creature with many legs. They're laughing about something. I make a mental note to learn some jokes so I can make them laugh when they come to my sleepover.

Autumn is still hiding behind her scarf. "Can we go in now? My legs are going numb."

"But we haven't come up with my sleepover theme. It has to be great. It has to be something the Haileys will remember. It has to make me seem . . . special."

"Then do something Hawaiian," she says.

I jump to my feet. Of course. I'm the only Hawaiian kid at my school. "A luau! That's what I'll do. I can get plastic leis and grass skirts at the dollar store. And we can eat roast pork and sweet rice and put straws into pineapples. You're a genius, Autumn!"

Our principal pokes her head out the office door. "Hey, you girls come in before you freeze to death!"

"Finally, a voice of reason," Autumn says, then hurries inside.

As the planning committee adjourns, a snowflake lands on my nose. I have a theme.

What could be better than Hawaiian sunshine in the middle of a Seattle winter?

This is going to be perfect.

The Boy Who Is Still
So Very Rude

When I get home from school, I step into the elevator like I always do and push button number six. And right behind me comes the boy from the third floor. *William.* I narrow my eyes at him, just to let him know that I haven't forgotten how he ignored me the last three times. But he doesn't look at me. He sets his cat carrier on the floor, pushes button number three, then sticks his hands into his pockets and stares at the wall. His red plaid coat is way too big and hangs past his knees. And his hat is made of fur. It looks real shabby.

I decide to give him another chance. Because I really don't want to feel like this every time I see him. Maybe he didn't mean to be rude. Shy people take time to warm up. "Are you stalking me?" I joke.

He doesn't answer.

"I'm just saying, it's weird that you always need to take the elevator at the *exact same time* I need to take it." I smile at him, but he doesn't look at me. The elevator doors close. "Is your cat a boy or a girl?"

He doesn't say anything.

"What's its name?"

Nothing.

I try to look into the carrier. I see a pair of yellow eyes and some black fur, but then William steps in front of it, blocking my view.

"Did you just take your cat for a walk or something?"

He pulls his hat down so it covers his eyes. Okay, now, that was definitely rude. What's he going to do next? Put his fingers in his ears so he doesn't have to hear me?

"Whatever." I open a pack of gum, but I know better than to offer him a piece. "I'm just trying to make conversation. 'Cause it's a polite thing to do."

The elevator stops, and the doors open. William picks up his carrier and steps off. I'm so glad we didn't get stuck. Our elevator has gotten stuck seven times already this year. I've never been in it when it happens, but the way things are going, I figure the odds are in my favor and I'll get stuck one of these days. And I'll have to wait for the fire department. But the last person in the world I want to be stuck with is the boy from the third floor.

I'd rather be stuck with farty old Todd, and that's the truth.

William walks off down the hall. "I hope your cat gives you fleas," I mutter under my breath. But then I lean out the door, just in case he whispers again. Which he does!

"She's a girl and her name is Belle."

The elevator doors close.

Helmet Head

I look up the name *William*, and then I read that it comes from the Germanic name Willahelm, which basically means "helmet protector of the head." Weird. Maybe that's why the boy from the third floor is so rude, because he never protected his head with a helmet and he has brain damage or something. "It's definite," I tell Mom. "I don't like him and I never will."

Mom is making dinner before she leaves for work. Tutu's recipe box is open, and one of the cards is out. Each card has a handwritten recipe surrounded by a red-checkered border. My favorites are baked mahimahi with potato chip crumbs and upside-down pineapple cake. But Tutu's favorites are manapua, which is a steamed white bun filled with barbecued pork, and haupia, which is coconut pudding cut into squares. "Why don't you like him?" Mom asks.

"He never talks to me when we're in the elevator."

"Maybe he's shy. He's just moved to a new neighborhood. That can be scary."

"He ignores me on purpose. I hate him."

"Hatred is like a volcano," Tutu says. She's sitting at the kitchen table in her pink bathrobe, slicing a cucumber.

I close my math book. "I thought hatred was like a pimple."

"Hatred is like many bad things. If you let hatred into your heart, it will fill you, like molten lava. Like Kilauea." Tutu lays the perfect slices on a plate, then drizzles salad dressing over them. "Then *boom*."

Mom pours three glasses of apple juice. "I'm sure Leilani doesn't actually *hate* this boy. Maybe he doesn't speak English."

"He speaks it," I say. "But only after he's disappeared down the hall." I tap my pencil on the table. "He's the rudest person I've ever met."

Mom puts the apple juice jug back in the refrigerator, then pulls a chicken casserole from the oven. "Methinks she doth protest too much."

"What does that mean?" I ask.

"It's William Shakespeare. It means that when you keep saying you don't like someone, you probably actually like that person."

"What?" I practically fall off my chair. "That's so not true. If I say I don't like him, I don't like him. Besides, Shakespeare never met the boy on the third floor, 'cause if he had, he wouldn't like him, either." I nearly snap my pencil in two. *Methinks she doth protest too much*? Maybe *William* Shakespeare hadn't worn a helmet, either.

"Okay, let's change the subject," Mom says. She sets the casserole on the table and we help ourselves. It's one of my favorites. The chicken thighs are cooked with broccoli and cream of mushroom soup and topped with a mess of cheese. "How was school today?"

I spoon sticky rice onto my plate. "Great. I have a theme for my sleepover. Hawaiian luau." I smile at Tutu, pretty sure she'll be proud of my choice.

"I'm not cooking," she reminds me.

"No problem. I can do it. I've already learned most of your recipes."

Mom pats my knee. "Make me a grocery list and I'll do whatever I can to help."

"Okay, but first I need to send out the invitations."

"Are you going to invite just girls? Or girls *and* boys?"

Tutu scowls. "Boys? Why would she invite boys? That's trouble if you ask me."

"Oh, Tutu, it's no big deal," Mom says. "Leilani's friends aren't in the dating stage yet, so I was just thinking it might be nice if she invited her cousin Todd."

"No way! Not Todd!" As I push back my chair, the table jiggles, nearly toppling everyone's juice.

"Leilani, calm down." Mom butters a slice of bread. "I just thought . . . well . . . I guess he's been having a hard time lately, and it would be nice to include him. That's all."

Hard time? What does that mean? He doesn't seem like he's having a hard time. For a nanosecond, I think about inviting Todd, but then I picture all the Haileys running from the apartment, chased by a big green fart cloud. "Please don't make me invite him. He's loud and pushy, and he farts on purpose. He's constantly trying to embarrass me."

She sighs. "It was just a suggestion."

We don't talk much after that. Mom has to eat quickly so she won't be late for her shift. "Thanks for watching Leilani," she says to Tutu. Then she grabs her purse, kisses my cheek, and whispers in my ear, "And thank you for watching Tutu."

Mom and I have an understanding. Although Tutu

thinks she's taking care of me, I'm actually taking care of her. She walks to the market every day, but she doesn't do much else on her own. If she falls asleep on the couch, I cover her with a blanket and turn down the volume on the TV. When she gets ready for bed, I remind her to take her medication. I'm the one who checks to make sure the stove is off and the heat is turned down and the door is locked before going to sleep. But Mom always thanks Tutu for watching me. I think she wants to make Tutu feel useful.

Another one of my chores at night is kitchen cleanup, so while Tutu watches *Wheel of Fortune* in the living room, I fill the dishwasher and turn it on. Then I water the fern that Mom keeps on our windowsill. That's when I see William. We have one tiny window in our kitchen, and it looks down into the alley that runs between our building and a dry cleaner's. It's not much of a view, so I never look out there. But William's red plaid coat catches my eye. I open the window and stick out my head. He's standing in the alley, holding a pair of scissors.

I can't help it. I have to know. "What are you doing?" I call.

He glances up.

"It's me, from the elevator," I tell him.

He pulls his fur hat over his eyes, then darts out of view.

THAT'S IT!

I've been super nice to him, and he's been the absolute rudest! My blood is boiling, like lava in Kilauea. "I swear . . ." I clench my fists. "I swear I will never talk to the boy on the third floor again." And since I want to make it official, I look up at the ceiling. "Do you hear me, God? Never! Again!"

"When you're done talking to God, I'd like a cup of tea!" Tutu hollers.

I set the kettle on the stove. Then I grab a pencil and a piece of paper from the junk drawer and start an extremely important list. The most important list I've ever made.

DO NOT invite to my sleepover.

1. William, the rude boy from the third floor!
2. Todd Burl, no matter what Mom says!

Manga Girl

Manga Girl almost always sits alone at school. I don't know if that's because she doesn't have friends or because she wants to sit alone. I'm so glad I've got Autumn to sit with. And Autumn is never sick, so I never have to eat alone.

Mom says there's nothing wrong with eating alone. Or going to the movies alone. She says that we have to be happy spending time with ourselves because the most important person in the world who should like you is yourself.

I like myself, but I still don't like eating alone.

I secretly call her Manga Girl because she wears these hats with ears, like cat ears or fox ears. Sometimes there's a cape attached to the hat. When she runs, she puts her arms behind her and says, "Whoosh." I'm not making that up. *Whoosh.* Like she's in a cartoon. I asked her once, "How come you say 'whoosh' when you run?" You know what she said? She said that if I had to ask that question, then I didn't know anything about manga. I know a little about manga, but I'm not a fan. It feels weird to read a book backward. I have enough trouble reading them forward.

I've never asked her why she wears the hats because, well, I think the answer might be kind of creepy. Jeremy Bishop told me that she's hiding a deformed ear. And someone else started a rumor that she has horns. No one really knows what's wrong with her head, but it must be bad because she never takes off the hats. After she'd been at our school for a few weeks, I started to feel sorry for her, so I invited her to sit with me and Autumn at lunch. She said she wanted to draw instead.

Manga Girl always sits in the corner. And she draws all the time. Our teacher, Mr. Pine, tells her to put away her sketchbook, but as soon as we have free time or reading time, she starts drawing again. She draws during lunch. And at break. But she never lets anyone see what she's drawing. I've tried, lots of times, but she always covers the page. I think that's why she chooses corners, because no one can sneak up and see.

Her real name is Tanisha Washington. *Tanisha* isn't

in my name book, so I looked it up online and found a bunch of different definitions. But a few places agreed that Tanisha is an African name that means "one who is born on Monday." A lot of people don't like Mondays because it means the weekend is over. But the day I don't like is Thursday because that's the day I have to leave class at eleven thirty to go to Reading Lab. According to my test results, I'm reading below grade level. The first day I had to go, Mr. Pine stopped right in the middle of his lesson on Washington state history, looked at the clock, and said, "Leilani and Stuart, it's time for you to *go to Reading Lab.*"

"I know," I said, gritting my teeth. Why did he have to announce it?

To make matters worse, Hayley Ranson and Heyley MacDonald are also in Mr. Pine's class. They sit side by side in the front row. Other than Autumn, they get the best grades in class. I know this because whenever we get homework back, I have a perfect view, from the fourth row, of the red *A*'s on their papers. I don't want to give them any reason to think I'm not smart enough to be in their group, so I make sure to watch the clock and jump out of my chair a minute before I'm supposed to leave for Reading Lab so that Mr. Pine won't make another announcement. Then I hurry toward the door, avoiding the front row so Hayley and Heyley won't notice me leaving.

But today I get distracted because I'm trying to figure out what my sleepover invitations will look like. Should they be shaped like the state of Hawaii? Or like a hula girl? Or maybe a pineapple?

"Leilani?" Mr. Pine calls from his desk. "It's time to—"

I drop my pen. *No no no no no no no. Don't say it!*

"—go to *Reading Lab*."

"Ugh," I grunt. Stuart's already left. Autumn smiles at me and waves good-bye. As I grab my folder, Manga Girl looks up from her drawing. Why is she staring at me? Hayley and Heyley turn and watch me leave. This is not how I want to be noticed.

When I get back from Reading Lab, everyone is heading for the cafeteria. "How'd it go?" Autumn asks as she pulls her Tupperware box out of her backpack.

"The usual," I say with a shrug. The usual is sitting with Stuart, working on vocab cards.

I glance over at Manga Girl. She's still sitting at her corner desk, huddled over her drawing. She looks at me, her eyes squinty beneath the brim of her cat hat. She draws. Then she looks at me again. Then draws some more. Then looks at me.

Wait a minute! Is she drawing *me*?

I need to see that drawing. But I have to be sneaky. If I startle her, she'll bolt. If she catches me looking, she'll crumple the paper. She'd rather eat her drawing than let me see it. So I pretend I need to wash my hands at the sink, and then I lunge sideways.

And I see it.

She's drawn a cartoon of a girl who has long black hair like mine. The girl is being attacked by gigantic letters, *A*, *B*, and *C*.

"That's mean," I say.

"It's not mean."

"It is. You're making fun of me."

"It's not done," she grumbles. Then she shoves the paper into her backpack and *whoosh*es out of the room.

"What was that about?" Autumn asks. I tell her what I saw. "I'm sure it wasn't you."

"Of course it was me. She was totally making fun of me going to Reading Lab."

"But why would she do that?" Autumn asks as we start down the hall. "Reading is all about wiring, not intelligence. A lot of famous people had trouble reading when they were young. Thomas Edison and Walt Disney both had dyslexia. And Einstein didn't get good grades. And George Washington couldn't spell at all."

Autumn could have told me that all those people

had also gone to Reading Lab, but it wouldn't have made me feel any better. That cartoon really stung.

When I get home, I add another name to the list.

DO NOT invite to my sleepover.

1. William, the rude boy from the third floor!
2. Todd Burl, no matter what Mom says!
3. Tanisha Washington, the Manga Girl!

The Story of Soup

After dinner, I make another list. I check the names in the school directory because the spelling is so confusing.

DO invite to my sleepover.

1. Hailey Chun
2. Haighley Brown
3. Hayley Ranson
4. Heyley MacDonald
5. Heeyley Kerrigan
6. Heighleigh Garfinkel
7. Autumn Maxwell

Then I grab some glue sticks, construction paper, markers, and a pair of scissors and dump them onto the coffee table. No way am I going to send free e-mail invites. This calls for the real thing.

"Why are you making such a mess?" Tutu complains. She's settled on her end of the couch, watching a game show called *Name That Tune*. It's an old show from when my mom was little. The way it works is that the band plays a few notes, and the contestants try to guess the song.

"I'm making the invitations for my Hawaiian luau sleepover," I tell her. "They're going to be pineapples."

Tutu grunts. "Pineapples aren't native to Hawaii. They were brought to the islands by the Spanish. Most everything was brought to Hawaii. Pigs, mongooses, rats—they all came by ship."

"What, like on a cruise ship?" I imagine a pig, a mongoose, and a rat sitting in deck chairs, which makes me laugh.

Tutu looks at me over the rims of her cat-eye glasses. "Listen up and you will learn. The only native mammal was the ʻōpeʻapeʻa, the hoary bat. And the only native food was kalo, the wild sweet potato."

I'm never sure if Tutu's stories are real or not. But this time it doesn't matter, because I have no idea how to draw a hoary bat or a wild sweet potato. "Thanks, but I think I'll stick with a pineapple."

So I cut the yellow shapes, glue them onto the paper, then cut out the green leaves and glue those on.

While I'm creating my masterpieces, Tutu shouts at the TV. "'Don't Sit Under the Apple Tree'!" "'Blue Moon'!" "'Jailhouse Rock'!" I don't know any of those songs. When *Name That Tune* is over, she points at the coffee table. "What's that?"

"My invitation list," I explain. "Those are the girls I'm inviting."

She wiggles her fingers. I hand her the list. She holds the paper real close and squints. "And who, exactly, are these girls?"

"Just some girls from school. And Autumn."

"I don't know these girls from school. What makes them so important that they get to be at your party?"

"Well . . ." I set the scissors back in their plastic case. "I want them to be my new friends. When Autumn visits her dad, I don't have anything to do. I get bored."

"Bored?" She snorts. "When I was a girl, there was no time to be bored. I had to pull weeds in my mom's garden, then pick the watercress and take it down to the market. I had to feed and water the chickens, and rake their pen, and I babysat my little brothers and helped my mom cook dinner. We had to wash our clothes by hand, so every week I washed my brothers' best shirts for Sunday church."

Sometimes Tutu's childhood sounds magical, but most of the time it sounds really hard. "I'm sorry you had to do all that," I say, "but my situation is totally different." Doesn't Tutu realize that I only have one true friend at school? And that having more would be great? "The Haileys have a lot of fun together. They have parties every weekend. The best parties. Everyone wants to go, but they only invite each other. If they come to my sleepover, and see that I'm just as fun as they are, then they'll like me, and I'll get invited to their parties."

"What about Autumn?"

"I'd only go on the weekends when Autumn has to stay at her dad's. Besides, Autumn wouldn't want to go to a Hailey party. She doesn't like parties. But she'll eat lunch with us."

"Maybe she will and maybe she won't. Autumn is a wise girl." Autumn and Tutu are close because Autumn comes over all the time. Since Autumn's grandparents live in California and she rarely gets to see them, Tutu is like a grandmother to her. "One day, Autumn will bloom like an ohia flower."

"She'll eat lunch with me and the Haileys," I say with

absolute confidence. Autumn and I are inseparable—except for every other weekend.

Tutu hands the list back to me. Then she grabs her clicker and mutes the TV. She doesn't do that very often, and it means she's going to tell me one of her stories.

"If you want to impress these girls, then you should make sleepover soup," she says.

Soup? Who eats soup at a party? I imagine the disappointed looks on their faces. "That's an interesting idea." I smile politely. "But I'm going to stick with my luau theme."

"That's too bad," she says with a shake of her head, "because sleepover soup is blessed by the Hawaiian gods. By Kāne, Lono, Kū, and Kanaloa. And if your guests eat the soup, their wishes will come true."

"Huh?" I'm intrigued. I sit on the couch. "What do you mean? How can gods bless soup?"

Tutu gets that dreamy look, as if she's standing back on her island, her toes in the sand, smelling the salt water. "It's a special recipe, handed down from generation to generation, from mother to daughter since sleepovers began."

I'm pretty sure I know all of Tutu's recipes. I've read through her cards, and Mom and I have cooked most of the dishes. But this one is new to me.

She sets the clicker aside and folds her hands. "You start with a pot of simmering chicken broth. This was easy to make back home because most everyone had a spare rooster running around or an old chicken that didn't lay eggs anymore. You cut off the chicken's head and—"

"Gross," I say.

"It's not gross, Leilani. How do you think chicken broth is made?"

"Mom always buys it in a can."

She sighs. "Yes, but fresh is better."

"You want me to kill a chicken? I'm not doing that. No way."

"Perhaps that is asking too much." She reaches out and pats my hand. "Clearly, you are too busy to cook soup that makes dreams come true." Then she takes one of the butterscotch candies from the candy bowl, unwraps it, and begins to eat it. She reaches for the clicker.

"Wait, Tutu. How does it make wishes come true?"

She raises her eyebrows. They were drawn on with a black eyeliner pencil. "Well, after you have a pot of chicken broth, you want to make sure it's on a gentle, welcoming simmer. You don't want hot broth splattering your guests." She rolls the candy around in her mouth. "Then each guest collects one ingredient for the soup. It must be a special ingredient, something that is mean-ingful to each person and comes from a special place. I always brought taro root."

"Why?"

"Because my grandfather owned a small taro farm. Did you know that taro was important to all Hawaiian people? It was so important that the word for family, *'ohana*, comes from *'ohā*, which are the shoots of the taro plant. You see? Just as the shoots come from the taro, we come from our families. And taro is important because all plant life in Hawaii is considered sacred. Taro is alive with *mana*."

While I've heard about mana, which is a kind of energy that Hawaiians believe you can find in just about everything, I've never heard anything about sleepover soup. That butterscotch candy smells really good. I grab one. "What about the gods?" I ask. "Where do they come in?"

Tutu closes her eyes, and I guess she's imagining her sleepover, way back when she was a little girl. Did they have sleeping bags? Did they play Truth or Dare?

"One by one, the guests add their special ingredients to the broth," she continues. "After everything has been added, you take the pot outside and stir it in the moonlight. A full moon is best, but any moonlight will do. Then you ask Hina-i-ka-malama to bless the soup."

That name sounds familiar, but I can't remember why. "Who's Hina-i . . . ?"

Tutu's eyes slowly open. She turns and scowls at me. "Hina-i-ka-malama. Do you never listen? Hina-i-ka-malama means 'Hina in the moon.' She grew tired of the islands, so she took the rainbow path to the sun. Finding the sun too warm, she climbed instead to the moon. If you look carefully, you can see her watching over travelers on Earth."

I nod as the story comes back to me. "So what happens then, with the soup?"

"Then you each take a sip. That is the important part. Only in the sharing will the magic be unleashed."

She turns away and unmutes the TV. *Jeopardy!* is on.

The soup sounds kind of cool. Blessed by a goddess who lives in the moon. I imagine moonbeams touching the soup, filling it with magic. Of course, it's one of Tutu's crazy stories and there's no way eating soup would make my wish, which is to become a member of the Haileys, come true. Besides, the Haileys are used to amazing sleepovers, and dumping a bunch of things into a pot of chicken broth is *not* amazing.

I stack the invitations next to the "DO invite" list. But I can't find any envelopes. "Tutu, when you go to the market tomorrow, can you get me some envelopes?" I ask. "So I can mail these?"

"Envelopes," she says with a nod. "Okay."

"Thanks, Tutu." I kiss her cheek. Her skin smells like coconut. *"Aloha pō."* That means "good night."

"Aloha pō."

Before I go to bed, I turn off the light, then look out the window. The man with the white beard is watching TV. The Croatian ladies have gone to bed. Hailey Chun's apartment is also dark, the drapes closed. She'll be so surprised when the invitation comes.

The snow didn't stick around, which is pretty typical for Seattle. I look up at the sky. There's no moon tonight, just a bunch of dark clouds. Good thing I'm not trying to make sleepover soup.

Tutu makes up the weirdest stories.

The Wrong List

When I get home from school the next day, I look over my shoulder to make sure William isn't coming down the street. But even if he gets into the elevator and even if he ignores me, it won't ruin my mood. I'm excited because I'm going to mail my invitations. I'm not even upset that the Haileys all wore red sweaters today and, even with my eavesdropping, I'd somehow missed this plan. Soon I'll be included in all their conversations.

Tutu is sitting at the kitchen table, eating an orange. Her lips glisten with juice. She nods at me.

"Hi, Tutu. Did you get the envelopes?" If I write the addresses on them real quick, I can run downstairs and get them in the slot before the 4:15 p.m. pickup.

"Sure, no problem."

"Thanks. Where are they?"

"I mailed them." She tears off another slice. Juice sprays across the table.

"You mailed them?" I freeze.

"Yes. I *mailed* them." She says this loudly, as if I can't hear very well.

"Really? You used my list?"

"Yes, the list. What's the big deal? I know how to look up an address and mail a letter. I'm not *that* old."

I dump my backpack onto the floor, then rush into the living room. Four pineapple invitations sit on the coffee table. "Tutu?" I pick them up and hurry back to the kitchen. "How come four didn't get mailed? I made seven invitations. One for each guest."

"No," she says.

"What do you mean, no?"

"Three guests. Three invitations."

Three guests? Maybe she hadn't worn her glasses.

"I delivered one in person. Why waste a stamp when the address is downstairs?"

"Downstairs?" I'm starting to get a weird feeling in my stomach, like I swallowed a rock. "You mean across the street, right? Hailey Chun lives in the condo across the street."

"No." Tutu finishes the orange, then gets up to wipe

her hands on a dish towel. "I put two in the mailbox and took one downstairs to the third floor."

Third floor?

"When I was a little girl, we had only one mail truck. It took a week to get a letter from one end of the island to the other. You could deliver it faster by walking."

Third floor!

"You want some apple juice?" She opens the refrigerator.

I dart back into the living room, and that's when I find it, lying on the sofa, next to Tutu's cat-eye glasses. The "DO NOT invite" list with three names. "Tutu, what did you do?" I cry.

There's no time to wait for the elevator. I run down the stairs as fast as I can. "No, no, no," I chant the whole way. All my hard work. My plans. What if Todd and Manga Girl and William get those invitations? No, that isn't going to happen. I can still save my sleepover. "No, no, no." But it's too late. The mail lady came early. I run outside and look up and down the sidewalk, just in case she's still around. She isn't.

AHHHHHHH!

I run back upstairs. When I burst into the kitchen, I can barely breathe. Mom is pouring a cup of coffee.

"Leilani?" she gasps. "Your face is all red. What's going on? What's happened?"

"Tutu . . ." I can't get the words out. "Tutu . . ."

Tutu scowls at me.

"Tutu . . . Tutu sent the invitations to the wrong people!" I hold the list up to Mom's face. "This is my 'DO NOT invite' list!"

"Leilani, calm down. I can't read it when it's pressed against my nose. Give me that." She takes it from me. "I don't understand. Why would you make a 'DO NOT invite' list? That seems so mean."

"It's not mean. No one was going to see it." I grab the "DO invite" list off the coffee table. "This is the right list. See? It says 'DO invite.' That one says 'DO NOT invite.' *NOT!*"

Tutu is seated at the table again, drinking juice. She shrugs. "One little word."

"But it's an important word. It's one of the most important words ever. It completely changes a sentence!" Does Tutu need to go to Reading Lab? I pace back and forth, my heart pounding in my ears. "There's no way to get the invitations back. They're gone. What am I going to do?"

Mom isn't freaking out. She doesn't even seem concerned. "I'm sure it will be okay," she says as she stirs milk into her coffee.

"Okay?" I'm starting to spit. Starting to froth at the mouth like a crazy person. "We're talking about Todd. And Manga Girl. And that boy from the third floor. It won't be okay!"

"Leilani," Mom says, "stop shouting at us. Now sit down and take a deep breath."

I stop pacing. I sit. I take a deep breath. But oxygen never solves anything. It only makes me dizzy. "I'll have to uninvite them."

Mom frowns at me. "You can't do that, Leilani. You can't uninvite people. That would be rude."

"Then I'll tell them it's canceled. I'll—"

Someone knocks on the door. *Whoever it is, please go away. I'm in the middle of a crisis.*

Mom answers the door. "Oh, hello," she says. Though I can't see William's face, I catch a glimpse of his plaid coat. I don't want to talk to him, so I dart behind the door. "You're the boy from the third floor, right?" Mom asks. Of course, he doesn't say anything. "I'm sorry, but I can't remember your name."

"William," Tutu tells her. Then she shuffles back to the living room to watch TV.

"Well, it's nice to meet you, William. Are you here to see Leilani?"

I stay behind the door. Why is he here? Maybe he's

going to tell us that he can't come to the sleepover. That would be great.

But William doesn't say anything. His footsteps echo as he walks away. "Uh, okay, good-bye," my mom calls down the hall. Then she closes the door. She's holding a piece of paper. "He left you this note."

The piece of paper is folded four times, with my name on the front in very tidy handwriting. I unfold it.

> Dear Leilani,
>   Thank you for inviting me to your sleepover.
>   I have never been to a sleepover before.
>   I would be very happy to come.
>   Sincerely,
>   William Worth
>
> P.S. I have selective mutism.

"He's a mutant? Well, that explains everything."

Mom takes the note and reads it. "Not *mutant*, Leilani. Mutism. That means he doesn't talk."

"But I've heard him talk. He whispers when the elevator doors are closing."

"*Selective* mutism means he can't talk in certain situations."

"Why not?" I ask. "What's wrong with him?"

"I don't know. I'm not a psychiatrist. But you'll need to explain this to your other guests so William won't feel uncomfortable."

"What? No way. There won't be any guests because I'm not having this party."

Mom puts her hands on her hips and gives me that look that makes me feel bad about myself. "Leilani, I raised you to be kind."

"But—"

She keeps looking at me.

I groan.

Cancellation Policy

I stay inside all day Saturday, watching TV with Tutu and not doing much else. At noon, Autumn goes to Bellingham to visit her dad. Hailey Chun leaves at two fifty-five for the barbecue sleepover. It's a long day.

On Sunday, Mom and I take Tutu to get a pedicure. The lady files all the dead skin off Tutu's heels, then paints her toenails pink. "In Hawaii, my feet were always so pretty," Tutu says. "But now I have to wear socks, and I get ugly winter feet."

The lady tells us about a place in Japan where you stick your feet into a pool and tiny fish eat the dead skin right off your heels and toes.

"Let's get some of those fish," Tutu suggests.

"And where would we put them?" Mom asks.

"In the bathtub. Then I can have nice feet all the time."

Mom says she'll look into it, then she winks at me.

Yep, this is my exciting Sunday, talking about feet. But at least it's better than what's going to happen next weekend at my sleepover. The. End. Of. The. World.

On Monday at lunch, Autumn sips her juice box and calmly reminds me, "The world isn't coming to an end. Why don't you just cancel the sleepover?"

"Mom won't let me cancel. She said it would be rude. She said Todd is having a hard time and I should be nice to him."

Autumn stops sipping. Her eyes get even bigger. "What kind of hard time?"

"I don't know." I glance over at the basketball team's table and start to think about what might be wrong. He doesn't look sick. He doesn't look sad. In fact, he's laughing. Maybe he's getting bad grades. That wouldn't surprise me. It's possible that the trouble-with-reading gene runs in our family. I hope he doesn't end up in Reading Lab with me, because that room is super small.

Back to my sleepover issues. "I can't cancel the party by pretending to be sick, because Mom always knows when I'm faking."

"You could get an *actual* sickness," Autumn says. "The average flu virus only takes one to two days to spread. The common cold takes a bit longer, maybe three days. But that's still enough time." She starts chewing on her straw.

"How am I supposed to *actually* get sick?"

"You could inhale deeply after someone sneezes. Or touch public handrails and doorknobs and then pick your nose. Those are sure ways for a virus to enter your body."

"Sick for real?" It's an idea. How much do I want to avoid this sleepover? Is it worth snot running down the back of my throat, phlegm balls, and fever sweats?

Yes, it is!

Autumn tucks a curl behind her ear. "On second thought, there's the possibility that you could catch something terrible, like tuberculosis or Ebola, and those things can be lethal."

No, it isn't!

I'm eating the day's cafeteria special—chicken strips and french fries. I jab my fork into one of the strips. "There has to be a way to cancel the sleepover without a trip to the emergency room."

"Too bad you didn't include a cancellation policy on your invitation," Autumn says. "Something like, if unforeseen circumstances should occur, like Tutu mailing my invitations to the wrong list, then I reserve the right to cancel without further explanation." She giggles. But I'm not laughing. "Maybe it won't be so bad," she says sweetly.

"Not so bad? You couldn't find weirder guests if you tried. A girl who thinks she's living in a comic book, a boy who farts on command, and another boy who doesn't talk because he's got . . ." I try to remember what it's called.

"He's mute?"

"Yeah, that's it. It's called . . . selective mutism."

Autumn gasps. "Wow, really? *Selective?* So that means he's not mute all the time, which rules out a physical cause. But even though he *can* talk, he doesn't talk in certain situations. What kind of situations?"

I think about it. "Well, he doesn't talk to me face-to-face. He only whispers if he's far away and I can't see him."

"How interesting. I want to read about that."

"My mom said she'd get us tickets." The happy voice belongs to Haighley Brown, over at the big round table. My ears prickle and I lean sideways. "The concert is next month."

"I've never been to a real concert," Heeyley Kerrigan says.

"Me neither," says Heyley MacDonald. "This is going to be so much fun!"

"Our first rock concert," Hailey Chun squeals. "Together!" They all high-five.

I'm so totally bummed, I stop eavesdropping. Autumn starts nibbling around the edges of her crustless cheese sandwich. I'm not enjoying lunch because my stomach is churning. How do I cancel my sleepover without disappointing my mom and without hurting feelings?

"Hey, maybe I can go to Todd's and Manga Girl's houses and get their mail before they get it."

"That's called mail tampering, and it's a federal offense." Autumn dabs her mouth with a napkin. "Besides, it only takes a day to deliver a letter within the city. They probably got the invites on Saturday."

"But Todd and Manga Girl haven't RSVP'd." I sit up straight. "Wait a minute, what if they can't come? How great would that be? Then all I'd have to do is tell William that I've canceled, but I'll tell Mom that William canceled on me. She'll never know the truth because he *doesn't talk.*" *Brilliant!*

"I don't know," Autumn says. "You're not very good at lying."

This is true. Mom always says that I wear my emotions on my sleeve. That's a weird saying. I imagine a big frowning emoticon stuck to my shoulder.

"Would you like to go to the science center's human brain exhibit with me next week?" Autumn asks. "My mom said she'd get us tickets. They have actual brains on display, and you can take tests that measure your IQ and—"

"Hey, cuz." Todd stops at the table. He crushes his milk carton with one hand, then tosses it at the recycling bin. Perfect shot. "I got your invite. Sounds like fun. Gotta admit I'm surprised. I thought you didn't like me."

"What?" I fake shock. If I tell him the truth, he'll tell his mom and she'll tell my mom, and I'll get another lecture about being kind. "Why would you say that?"

He shrugs. "Just a feeling, I guess." He smiles at Autumn. "Hey, Autumn. Are you going to Leilani's sleepover?"

She turns red, nods, then starts nibbling real fast.

"Cool. See you Saturday." As he walks away, Autumn watches, her eyes as round as planets.

"Crud," I grumble.

"Whoosh." It's Manga Girl. She's left her corner and is standing in the exact spot where Todd was just standing. She tucks her sketchbook under her cape. "My dad said I have to go to your sleepover even though I don't want to. He said I need to work on my social skills." I don't know how she makes her cat ears wiggle, but she does. Then she darts away.

I slump in my chair. How could things get worse?

"I'm not doing anything this Saturday." This time it's Hayley Ranson who's talking.

"Me neither," says Heyley MacDonald.

I can't believe it. They have *no* plans. That means that if they'd gotten my invitations, they would have said yes!

Autumn leans close to me and whispers, "You could still give them invites."

Autumn is usually brilliant, but I only need a nanosecond to realize that this is a *terrible* idea. "I can't have them come to a party with William, Todd, *and* Manga Girl. They'll think I have weird friends. They'll think *I'm* weird."

Autumn shrugs. "Everybody's a *little* weird."

"The Haileys aren't weird," I whisper back. "They're totally normal."

Over at the big round table, Hailey Chun makes an announcement. "Since there's nothing else going on, let's do a sleepover this Saturday," she says. "At my house."

The Haileys cheer.

Autumn pushes her lunch aside and gives me a hug.

Friday Night

It's Friday night, less than twenty-four hours before doomsday. "What are you doing in bed already?" Mom asks.

"I'm sick."

"Uh-huh."

I can tell by her tone she isn't buying my lie. But I figure I might as well give it a try. What do I have to lose? "My stomach hurts. And my head hurts. My back hurts, too. We had to play crab hockey in gym, so I think I pulled a bunch of muscles." The crab hockey part is true. Autumn and I and the rest of the class had been forced to scuttle sideways on the disgusting gym floor. "I got kicked in the knees, like, a million times. I'm so sore there's no way I can do a sleepover."

Mom raises an eyebrow.

I sense I'm going to lose this battle. I cross my arms. "This is all Tutu's fault."

"Maybe," Mom says. She sits on my bed and lowers her voice. "But we have to understand that Tutu is getting old, and sometimes she gets confused. She'd never hurt you on purpose. She loves you very much. When your dad died, she was the first to fly from Hawaii. She held you during the entire funeral."

I'd never heard that before. "I know she loves me. But this is still her fault."

"Well, maybe you should recognize that it's also your fault. Maybe you shouldn't have made that list."

We both go quiet for a moment. "Yeah, maybe you're right about that." I would feel pretty bad if someone put my name on a "DO NOT invite" list.

She sighs. "I spoke with William's mother yesterday. She's a very nice lady. Did you know you two have something in common?"

I shake my head. What could we possibly have in common? I don't own a giant plaid coat. I don't carry a cat around in a cat carrier. And I like talking to people face-to-face. In fact, my teachers often say that I talk *too* much.

"His father died when he was a baby."

I grimace. That's a cruddy thing to have in common.

"She told me that William's been homeschooled because of his mutism. He's had trouble making friends. She said he was starting to show some improvements, but then recently, something set him back."

Is she trying to make me feel sorry for William? Well, I am sorry that he lost his dad, and I am sorry that he can't talk. But when it comes right down to it, everyone has problems. Including me. I only have one friend, and even though she's my best friend and I don't want to trade her, I'd like to have a few more friends. Hailey friends.

"William's mom thinks the sleepover will be good for him. To be with other kids."

I tighten my arms and clench my jaw. My mom is real good at the whole guilt thing. I wonder if William actually wants to come to my sleepover, or if his mom is just like my mom and is making him do it. Something else we'd have in common.

She pats my leg. "I just want you to know, Leilani, that by being nice, you can change someone's life."

I already know that. But the sleepover is supposed to be about changing *my* life, not William's.

Mom smiles sweetly at me. I'm stuck. There's no

getting out of this party. "I'll bring you some Tylenol for those aching muscles, and I'm sure you'll feel much better by morning." She starts to leave but turns in the doorway. "Make a list of the food you need, and we'll go shopping tomorrow."

"I don't care about the food," I say, disappearing under my quilt.

"But you wanted to do a Hawaiian luau."

"Not anymore."

"What do you mean, not anymore?" She tries to pull the quilt down, but I grip it and hold it over my head. "Leilani, you're acting like a brat."

"I don't care."

"Well, you need to feed your guests. How about hot dogs and macaroni salad? And ice cream?"

"No!" I cry. "Ice cream makes Todd fart. No ice cream!"

"You are *so* cranky," Mom says. "Sometimes I think you and Tutu are the same person."

Before she leaves for work, she tells me to check my attitude and send it somewhere far away, because no daughter of hers is going to act like a drama queen.

I decide to stay under my quilt for a while, thinking things through. There's got to be a way to get out of this party, but I don't get any lightbulb ideas. What if I stayed in bed all weekend, like a protester? I could even make a sign.

"Get the phone!" Tutu hollers from the living room. She never answers our phone. It can ring a million times and she still won't move. "Get the phone! I'm busy!"

"I'm busy, too!" I holler back.

"I'm busier! I'm watching *The Price Is Right*!"

"What's so busy about that? I'm protesting my life!"

"What do you mean, you're protesting your life? You have a good life! You have hot water and a flushing toilet. Now answer the phone!"

I stomp down the hall.

"Hello?"

It's Autumn. "Hi, Leilani. Whatcha doing?"

"Playing sick," I confess. "But it's not working."

"Oh, I'm sorry. Well, I've been reading about selective mutism, and it's really interesting. It's rare, but most of the cases occur in kids who feel really anxious."

I glance out the kitchen window. Even though it's dark outside, the dry cleaner's sign is lighting the alley. William's standing down there, his coat buttoned up to his chin. Using a pair of scissors, he snips a few stalks off a scraggly weed. Why's he doing that? I think about opening the window and asking, but I know he won't answer.

"Leilani?" Autumn says.

"Yeah?"

Then she asks a question that makes me shiver. "Why do you think William feels so anxious? Do you think something terrible happened to him?"

"Well, his dad died."

"Oh, that's so sad."

Why is William cutting weeds with scissors? I can't figure it out. Autumn's mother tells her it's time for bed, so we say good-bye.

"Who was that?" Tutu hollers because the TV volume is so loud.

"Autumn!" I holler back

"I like Autumn! One day she is going to bloom like an ohia flower!"

"Yeah, I know!"

I stomp back to my room.

12

Waiting Is the Hardest Part

It's Saturday morning. Doomsday has arrived.

Mom's asleep, so I creep into the kitchen. I fill a bowl with Cheerios and milk, then sit at the table. I feel jittery. Antsy. I glance at the clock.

When I was eight years old, I went to an orthodontist to get two teeth pulled. I started to cry in the waiting room. I kept imagining all sorts of horrid things, like superlong needles and gushing blood. Mom told me that the waiting was the worst part, but it would soon be over and then I'd never have to get those teeth pulled again. She was right. When it was over, I felt so much better, and life went back to normal.

Relief washes over me as I realize that the same will be true about this sleepover. On Sunday morning, it will be over. Todd, Manga Girl, and William will leave, and I'll never have to do it again.

And then I can set a new date and send out invites to the "DO invite" list and have the *real* sleepover—the one that matters. The one that will change my life. The sleepover I'll remember forever and ever.

I feel better. It's just one night. "I can do this," I whisper to myself.

I start eating the Cheerios, and that's when our apartment door opens and Tutu walks in with a bag of groceries. The bag is strapped to a little wheeled cart. She leans against the sink, struggling to catch her breath.

"Are you okay?" I grab a glass of water. "Here." She drinks it. "Why didn't you wait for me?" I usually walk to the store with her on the weekend.

"I got food. For your party."

"Thanks, Tutu. I'll help unpack." I reach for the grocery bag, but Tutu blocks me with her arm.

"No," she says. "You go away. I will make the food." She unwraps her scarf and sets it on the counter. Then she takes off her hat and coat. She's wearing her favorite pink shirt, with lime-green embroidery.

"But you said you didn't want to cook."

"I changed my mind. You need Tutu's help."

"But—"

She wags a finger at me. "You *need* Tutu's help. Now go away so I can concentrate."

Suddenly, she seems to have a lot of energy. Her eyes kind of light up. Why is she so excited about cooking? Even though she has all those recipes, she *never* cooks anymore.

"Yeah, okay." I don't ask what she's going to cook. It doesn't matter. I'm not trying to impress anyone at this sleepover. I imagine the sleepover ending early because Tutu hands out bowls of macadamia nuts and gives everyone diarrhea. Everyone except me and Autumn, of course.

I glance at the hall clock. Noon. Three hours to go. I call Autumn. "Please get here early."

"I'll try."

"I need you. It's going to be so awkward. What am I supposed to say? 'Hi, I know we're not friends and we never hang out, but welcome to my sleepover'?"

"That's sounds okay."

"Ugh. Just get here early. Please?"

I stay in my room for most of the afternoon, lounging on my bed, working on math homework. This is definitely worse than waiting for two teeth to get pulled. And to make things *even* worse, across the street, Hailey Chun is getting ready for *her* sleepover. At one fifteen, Hailey's mom vacuums the apartment. Groceries are delivered at two o'clock by a Safeway van. At two fifteen, Hailey's dad sets up the grill on the balcony, but then it starts to rain, so he covers the grill. Is the rain going to ruin Hailey's plans? What's her theme? I haven't figured that out yet.

At two twenty-five, Mom comes into my room. She's already in her scrubs. "I have to go in early and cover a shift," she explains. "I'm sorry I won't be here to greet your guests." Then she hugs me. "I know you don't want to do this, but you're being kind, and I'm very proud of you. Call me if you need anything. And try to be positive. Remember, it's all about attitude."

"Autumn would disagree with that statement," I tell her. "She'd say it's about facts. And the facts are, I have to entertain *and* spend the night with people I don't really like."

"Yes, but do you remember what Tutu always says? About sugarcane?"

One of Tutu's favorite stories is about how her dad would bring cane home from the fields. They didn't have money for fancy cakes or chocolates, but it didn't seem to matter much because Tutu and her brothers loved chewing on the cane. Her dad would cut foot-long sections, then skin them. They looked like ordinary sticks, but once she started chewing and gnawing, the sticks turned into something delicious.

"I'm just saying, Leilani, that you never know. Sometimes we judge things, or people, but if we give them a chance, they turn out to be sugar."

"Yeah, Mom, I get it." I sigh. "I already decided I'm going to have a better attitude about this."

She hugs me again. "Try to have fun. And I'll see you in the morning."

Right after Mom leaves, I call Autumn, but I get her voice mail. "Where are you? I need you!"

At two forty-five, the buzzer sounds, which means someone is waiting outside the building. Autumn is finally here!

"Get the door!" Tutu hollers. She's in her bedroom, watching TV. I think she's giving me privacy for my party. I wish she'd hang out in the living room, because that would take a lot of pressure off me. She could entertain everyone with stories about hoary Hawaiian bats.

It smells nice in the kitchen. A big pot sits on the stove.

BUZZ.

"Get the door!"

"Hi, Autumn," I say through the intercom.

"It's not Autumn," a girl answers.

I cringe. I want to say, *Go away, I'm sick, the sleepover's been canceled*. But instead I say, "Come on up."

Then I push the security button, which opens the building's front door.

Mom said it's all about attitude. Do we look at the sugarcane and see a brown stick? Or do we give it a chance and discover that it's actually sweet? I understand her point. But she's never had Manga Girl draw a mean picture of her. She's never been stuck in the elevator with William, or been trapped in one of Todd's fart clouds. I would try my best to have a good attitude, but facts are facts.

My guests are just a bunch of sticks.

I take a long breath. The sleepover disaster is about to begin.

The Most Unwanted Guests Ever

"Just so you know, I don't sleep much," Manga Girl tells me. "I'm nocturnal."

"Then why'd you bring a sleeping bag?" I ask.

She shrugs. "My dad made me." The sleeping bag is tucked under one arm, and a panda-shaped backpack hangs from her other arm. She's traded her cat-eared hat for a red hat with fox ears. A red cape is attached. She looks like Red Riding Hood. "Where do you want me to put this stuff?"

I point into the living room. She sets everything on the carpet, but of course she doesn't take off her fox hat and cape. She pulls her sketchbook out of her backpack, then pushes an armchair into the corner and sits. She doesn't ask if she can move furniture around. We stare at each other. Then she opens her sketchbook, takes a pen from her cape's pocket, and starts drawing.

Since we're alone, I figure this is the perfect time to tell her exactly how I feel.

"I want you to know that the cartoon you drew of me made me feel really bad." I stand still, waiting, thinking that she'll say she's sorry. But she doesn't say anything.

I shuffle in place. "I would probably feel better if you said you were sorry for drawing that cartoon."

She holds the sketchbook to her chest and narrows her eyes. "I think *you* should say *you're* sorry for sneaking a peek at my drawings. They're private."

"Private? The cartoon you drew is about *me*, and it's *my* life."

She shrugs. "It's social commentary. All cartoons are social commentary." Wow, this is not sounding like an apology, not one bit. I feel my cheeks go red.

"Yeah? Well, maybe I don't want to be part of your social commentary."

She taps her pen against the paper. "You don't get to choose who or what I draw, Leilani. I observe people, and some catch my interest and some don't. That's how I get my ideas. Besides, the cartoon isn't what you think it is."

I suppose I could be flattered. Manga Girl thinks I'm interesting enough to draw. But why did she have to draw the one thing that embarrasses me?

Someone knocks.

"Hey, cuz!" Todd says after I open the door. I think he's grown another foot since the last time I saw him. He's wearing his usual basketball shirt and shorts. "Some old guy let me into the building. Let's get this party started!" He marches into the living room and dumps his stuff. "Hey, Tanisha, you look like Red Riding Hood."

"I'm not Red Riding Hood."

"Well, you look like her." He scratches the back of his neck. "I didn't know you and Leilani were friends."

"We're not," she says quickly.

Todd smirks as if she's joking. "Ha, that's funny." He plops onto the couch. "You got chips or something?"

I'm not sure if we have chips. Tutu didn't let me unpack the groceries. I begin to search the pantry. There are no chips. I look in the refrigerator. No hot dogs or macaroni salad or sodas. What did Tutu buy?

"Here," I say, handing Todd a box of Cheerios. Thank goodness the Haileys aren't here to see my pathetic snack offering.

Todd doesn't seem to mind. "Cool." He shoves his hand inside and begins eating. He tries to get a look at

Manga Girl's drawing, but she blocks his view with her arm. "Hey, I've been meaning to ask you, what's the deal with your ears?"

Manga Girl's hand flies to the side of her head. "What do you mean?"

"Those hats, with the ears." He points at her. "How come you always wear them?" I take a deep breath. Will she tell us that something is wrong with her head? Are all those rumors true?

She closes her sketchbook. "I choose my ears based on my mood or my situation. Because I have never been here, and because Leilani and I barely speak at school, tonight will be a journey into the unknown. I figured I might need the powers of cunning and stealth, so I am *kitsunemimi*." She waits for us to nod or something, as if we know what she's talking about.

"Kitsu-what?" Todd asks. I'm glad I'm not the only one who is confused.

"*Kitsunemimi* is the name for a human with fox ears." She points to her red ears.

Todd frowns. "Wait, you and Leilani barely speak? So you really aren't friends?"

"That's right," she says.

Todd looks at me, and I know that the next question that pops out of his mouth will be, "Why did you invite someone who isn't a friend to a sleepover?" But telling the truth about the "DO NOT invite" list would hurt everyone's feelings, so I try to change the subject. "Speaking of fox ears, Todd's name means 'fox,'" I say.

"Seriously? I never knew that. Guess that makes me a *total fox*." He laughs and a Cheerio flies out of his mouth. "So, is this kitsu thing from one of those manga books? Like a superhero or something? Hey, I got a super-power. Wanna smell it?"

Yep, the whole night is going to be like this. Before Todd can fire his superpower, I retreat to the kitchen.

Where's Autumn?

BUZZ.

I run out the door, then pace in the hall, waiting for the elevator. When Autumn finally steps out, I hug her extra hard. "What took you so long? I need you. It's weirdo central in there."

"Traffic was bad," she explains as she wipes drops off her raincoat. Then she chews on her lower lip, looking nervously at the open door to my apartment. "Is Todd here?"

"Todd *and* Manga Girl." I groan. "I was trying real hard to have a good attitude about this, but I don't want to go back in there. She's going to draw mean cartoons all night, and he's going to stink up the place." I grab her arm. "What if we leave? I'm serious. We can go to your house. They can have the sleepover without us."

"Since I'm not a fan of parties, I would normally welcome your suggestion, but—" She stares over my shoulder. Todd barrels toward us and nearly knocks me over.

"Hi, Autumn." He smiles at her. A couple of Cheerios roll off his shirt.

"Hi," Autumn whispers. She begins to fidget.

Todd grabs her sleeping bag and backpack. "Hey, let me help you with these." As he carries them into the living room, Autumn and I follow. Guess he can have good manners when he wants to. "Autumn's here," he tells Manga Girl. She's hunched over her sketchbook, pen in hand.

I glance out the window. It's raining pretty hard. A taxi pulls up to the curb outside Hailey Chun's building. Heeyley Kerrigan gets out. The doorman holds the door as she hurries inside, sleeping bag in hand and a big smile on her face. It's painful to watch, but I can't help myself.

"Is anyone else coming?" Todd asks.

"No," I say, still gazing longingly at Hailey Chun's building.

"Yes, there is." Autumn nudges me with her elbow.

"Oh right, there is someone else." How can I explain the boy from the third floor? "He's new. He just moved into the building last month. His name is William. He's homeschooled."

"Homeschooled?" Todd grabs a couple of butterscotch candies. "How come?"

Autumn is standing real close to me. "Should we tell them?" she whispers.

"It's not a secret," I whisper back. "He wrote it on a note."

"What's not a secret?" Todd asks.

"William has this thing called selective mutism," I say.

Manga Girl stops drawing. Todd stops chewing. "Whoa, that's cool, I guess. Actually, I don't know. Selective *what*?"

I look at Autumn. "Can you tell them? You'll be able to explain it so much better." She grimaces, then swallows hard. She opens her mouth, as if to say something, then closes it. Her face gets red. Talking in front of a group is one of Autumn's least favorite things to do. I guess I wasn't thinking of Todd and Manga Girl as a group. "That's okay," I tell her. "I can—"

"Selective mutism is a very interesting condition," she blurts, stringing the words together real fast.

"Can you talk louder?" Manga Girl asks. "Even with my highly sensitive fox ears, I can barely hear you." Her little fox ears turn toward us. How does she do that?

Autumn clears her throat, but it doesn't make much difference. We all lean closer to hear. "Selective mutism is an inability to speak in a social setting, but the person can speak in other settings, like at home or when alone."

"So that means he's shy?" Todd asks.

"Not exactly," Autumn tells him. "Shyness isn't . . ." She pauses. "Shyness isn't . . ."

"Shy people can still talk," I point out. "I mean, Autumn's super shy, but she's talking to us right now." I pat Autumn on the back.

By the way Autumn is shuffling in place, I can tell she doesn't like all the attention. In a few more minutes, she'll probably have to rush off and use the bathroom.

Todd scrunches up a candy wrapper and tosses it into a vase. "Then if he's not shy, what's his deal? Is he stupid?"

I have no idea if William is stupid or not. But Autumn, who's never met him, is quick to jump to his defense. "Selective mutism is not about intelligence, or lack of intelligence. It's about anxiety. People who have it feel very anxious in certain situations, and that anxiety makes them unable to speak. It's not a choice." Sometimes Autumn sounds like she's ten years older than us.

Todd crinkles another wrapper, then tosses it at the cereal box. His aim is perfect. "Jeez, Leilani, why'd you invite a kid who doesn't talk?"

I still don't have an explanation. But luckily, I don't have to answer, because someone knocks on the apartment door.

"That's probably him," I say. Dread sweeps over me. Slowly, I walk toward the door, knowing that when I open it, the last guest will step through and the worst sleepover in the history of the world will officially begin. But what if I don't open it? Is it too late to end this?

You're being kind, and I'm very proud of you, Mom said.

I reach for the knob. Something feels different. I turn around. Manga Girl, Todd, and Autumn are standing right behind me, so close I can feel Todd's breath on my head. They're staring at the door as if some kind of prize is stashed behind it, like on *The Price Is Right*.

"Give me some room," I complain, jabbing Todd with my elbow.

He takes a step back.

Last week I stood in the kitchen and made a vow to

God that I would never speak to William again. But thanks to Tutu, I'm going to be stuck with him all night. What are we going to do? I didn't plan any games. Maybe we can play Scrabble. You don't need to talk during Scrabble. Or maybe we can just watch TV. That's it, we'll watch TV all night, and then nobody has to talk to anybody and we'll fall asleep and it will be over.

I like that plan.

Forcing a half smile, I open the door.

14

A Soup Mutiny

William Worth, the boy from the third floor, is wearing his gigantic plaid coat, scuffed leather shoes, and fur hat. He has a red sleeping bag and the suitcase I saw in the elevator, with the stickers all over it—Budapest, Toronto, Los Angeles. Why'd he bring such a big piece of luggage? Does he think he's staying more than one night?

"Hi," I say. That's about the best I can do. If one of the Haileys had been standing at the door, I would have squealed and bounced around. There would have been hugs and high fives. *Come in, come in, welcome to my home!* But my smile quickly fades, not that he notices, because he's staring at the floor.

The others press against me again, trying to get a good look. Todd practically pushes me out the door.

"Come on in," I say. Todd moves aside, making room for the new kid.

William drags his suitcase inside. Then he stands there. We're looking at him. He's looking at the floor.

"Okay, so who wants to watch TV?" I ask.

"TV?" Todd complains. "We can watch TV anytime. This is a party!" He holds out the cereal box to William. "Want some?"

William glances up, then lowers his eyes again.

This is going to be the longest night ever.

The door to Tutu's bedroom opens, and she shuffles out. Even though it's only three o'clock in the afternoon, she's in her pink bathrobe. "Hello, Autumn," she says. They hug. Then she shows Autumn her pink toenails. The polish has started to chip. "We're going to get fish for the bathtub so my feet will always look like this."

"That's nice," Autumn tells her.

Tutu looks at my other guests.

"Uh, everyone, this is my great-grandmother, Tutu," I say. "Tutu, this is Manga—I mean, Tanisha. This is William. And you already know Todd."

"Hi, Tutu," Todd says.

She glances at the Cheerio box in his hand, then scowls. "I'm not cleaning up after you." She points to Todd's feet, where he's dropped two Cheerios.

"Oops. Sorry." He bends down, picks them up, then eats them.

Tutu pushes her cat-eye glasses up her nose. "Okay, listen closely. I'm the chaperone tonight, so I want to make sure you understand the rules. First rule—no setting fire to anything. Second rule—no drinking alcoholic beverages or smoking anything at all."

"You don't have to worry. We wouldn't engage in any of those activities," Autumn assures her.

"I know *you* wouldn't, but these others look a bit wild." She wags a finger. "And third rule—boys and girls do not share sleeping bags."

"Tutu," I groan, my face heating up.

She sets her hands on her broad hips. "Any questions about the rules?" We all shake our heads. "Okay, then. Have fun. I'm going to be in my room." And off she goes, just like that.

Todd turns the Cheerio box upside down. "Hey, Leilani, it's empty. You got something else to eat?"

"You ate that whole box and you're still hungry?" I ask.

"I'm an athlete," Todd says, flexing his biceps. "I need fuel." He walks over to the stove and takes the lid off the pot. "This smells good. What is it?"

"Something Tutu made," I tell him.

"Can we eat it?"

"I don't know. I'll go ask."

If this were my *real* sleepover, I would serve Hawaiian punch in fancy cups with paper umbrellas. And I would put maraschino cherries in the ice cubes. And we'd have Hawaiian-style potato chips, which are thicker than regular potato chips. Tutu always says that any potato grown in the rich Hawaiian soil is better than all other potatoes because of that whole spirit-force thing. I think she totally made that up.

"Tutu?"

She grunts.

I open her door. She's propped up in bed, sitting in the dark, the light from the TV flickering on her face. "Are you okay? How come you're already in your bathrobe?"

"I'm a little tired, that's all. I might take a nap."

"Can I get you anything?"

"Not right now." She changes the channel.

"Um, Tutu? I was wondering, when you went to the store, what food did you get for the party? I can't find anything."

"I made chicken broth. For the sleepover soup."

"Huh?"

"Don't worry. I didn't cut off a chicken's head. It was already cut off."

"But I didn't want soup." I am beginning to think that Tutu has selective *hearing*.

"This is good Hawaiian soup. Now go. I can't hear my show. And close the door."

"But—"

"Leilani, I've been canning pineapple all day and I'm tired. Go." She thinks she's back in Hawaii, in the cannery. She does that sometimes.

In the kitchen, Manga Girl is sitting with her back against the wall, drawing. Todd and Autumn are at the table. William is standing, staring at the floor. No one is talking. We could be at a funeral, it's that much fun.

"So, it looks like we don't have anything to eat," I explain.

Manga Girl scowls at me. "But the invite said Hawaiian luau."

"Yes, well, I guess we're going to have a change of plans."

"Did you find out what's in the pot?" Todd is still holding the lid. Steam rises, carrying with it a lovely salty scent.

"It's nothing, just some chicken broth for a weird soup."

"You mean sleepover soup?" Autumn points to a card that is lying on the table. The card has a red-checkered border.

"Sleepover soup?" Todd asks. "What's that?"

"I don't know," I say with a shrug. "It's supposed to be an old Hawaiian tradition. Actually, I'm not even sure it's a tradition. Tutu makes up stories all the time. I mean, how can soup be magic?"

"Magic?" Manga Girl closes her sketchbook and leaps to her feet. Even William looks up. "Let me see that."

Todd, Autumn, and William crowd around Manga Girl as she holds the recipe card. She reads aloud.

Sleepover Soup

An ancient Hawaiian recipe handed down from generation to generation. If all directions are followed, this soup is guaranteed to grant wishes.

1. Begin with a pot of chicken broth simmering on the stove. If you don't like killing chickens, you can get the broth from a can, but it won't taste as good.

2. Each guest must gather a special ingredient for the broth. The special ingredient should come from a special place.

3. Once the ingredients are added, set the soup beneath the moonlight. Ask Hina-i-ka-malama to bless the soup.

4. Everyone makes a wish and takes a sip of soup. If all instructions are followed, the wishes will come true.

Important Note: The magic won't work unless everyone participates.

"Is this for real?" Todd asks.

"Of course it's not real," I say.

Manga Girl cocks her head. "How do you know?"

"I know because . . ." I don't want them to think that Tutu's crazy. "I think this is like wishing before you blow out a birthday candle. It's a nice idea, but there's no such thing as magic. Am I right?"

Todd shrugs. "Maybe, maybe not."

"What does she mean by a 'special ingredient'?" Manga Girl asks.

I try to remember what Tutu said. "I guess it's something that's important to you. And it comes from a place that's important to you. When Tutu was a little girl and she made the soup, she brought taro root because her grandfather owned a taro root farm."

Autumn's hand shoots into the air. Todd lowers his voice, to sound like an adult. "Yes, Miss Maxwell? Do you have a question?"

Autumn blushes and lowers her hand. "It's not a question. Actually, it's a statement." She steps closer to me. Her voice is still quiet. "I agree with Leilani. Magic doesn't exist. Besides, I don't see what kind of physical effect moonlight can have on soup. You can fry an egg on the concrete in sunlight, but moonlight doesn't heat things up. The moon doesn't actually produce light. Its light is a reflection from the sun."

"What if it's not scientific?" Manga Girl says. "What if the moon goddess has special powers?"

I shake my head. *We're not living in a comic book*, I want to say.

Autumn raises her hand again. "You don't have to do that," I whisper to her.

"Oh, right." She lowers her hand. "I'd like to point out that there's no evidence that gods or goddesses exist," she says, her usual rational self. "Therefore, I remain skeptical about the authenticity of the recipe. I say it's a work of fiction."

I put an arm around my best friend's shoulder. "Exactly what she said." But even though the debate seems to be over, we still have the problem of having no food. I look into the pot. The broth smells good, but broth is something you eat if you're getting over the flu—it isn't a real meal. I begin to feel bad about my lack of planning. "Look, guys, I guess this is all we have. Should we order a pizza?"

Among the five of us, we only have seven dollars and fifty cents. Tutu's turned off the TV, which means she's taking a nap, so I can't ask her for money. Without food, this night could drag on forever. I wonder if Mom will give us her credit card number so we can order over the phone. I'm about to call her when William clears his throat, startling everyone because it's easy to forget he's in the room.

He walks out of the kitchen, then steps into our coat closet and closes the door. What is he doing in there? We hear muffled sounds. "Did he just say something?" I ask.

Todd opens the door. "Did you say something?" William, who's standing between my mom's suede jacket and my raincoat, grabs the knob and closes the door again. More muffled sounds. Autumn, Manga Girl, Todd, and I press our ears to the door.

"Yeah, he said something," Manga Girl confirms.

"What did he say?" I ask.

"Dude, we can't hear you!" Todd hollers. "Talk louder!"

There's a pause. Then William's voice whispers, "I think we should make sleepover soup."

"Whoa," Todd says. "He *does* talk." He looks at Autumn. "What do you think, Autumn? Do you want to make the soup?"

"We . . ." She swallows hard. "We didn't bring special ingredients."

Todd smiles at her. "We could get them. We could go out right now, and get them."

"Like a scavenger hunt?" Manga Girl's fox ears twitch.

"Sure," Todd says.

Was this some kind of mutiny? What about my plans to sit around and watch TV and let the night pass quickly? "Are you suggesting we leave the apartment and go on a scavenger hunt to find ingredients for a recipe my grandmother made up that doesn't really work?"

"Yep."

I point toward the window. "But it'll be dark soon." One of the cruddy things about Seattle in winter is that it gets dark early.

"That won't be a problem because we'll be in a group," Todd says. "And we have bus passes, right?"

"I'm not supposed to leave the neighborhood," I tell him.

"Then we won't leave the neighborhood. We'll stay on Capitol Hill."

Both Manga Girl and Todd are smiling as if we already agreed to go on a scavenger hunt. But we haven't agreed on anything.

"Let's take a vote," Todd says. "If you wanna make the soup, then raise your hand." Todd raises his. Manga Girl raises hers. Autumn and I don't budge.

"Two to two is a tie," I say. "So we're not going."

"Wait, there's one more." Todd opens the closet door. "Yo, dude, how do you vote? Do you wanna go on a scavenger hunt and make sleepover soup?"

William steps out of the closet. He shuffles in place. He looks at the ceiling, then at the walls.

Then he raises his hand.

Todd punches a fist in the air. "The majority votes yes. Looks like we're going on a hunt. Who wants to go first?"

"It's Leilani's party," Autumn says. "Shouldn't . . . shouldn't she decide?"

Todd nods. "Yeah, I guess you're right." Everyone looks at me and waits.

I'm not sure what to say. Why am I so against making the soup? I know I'm being stubborn, but part of me doesn't want my sleepover to be fun. Todd, Manga Girl, and William are here because of a big mistake. I'm prepared to endure the night, like sitting in an oral surgeon's waiting room, and then it will be all over.

But the other part of me knows that a scavenger hunt would be entertaining. Even if the wishes don't come true, it would be something to do.

I look toward the living room. Hailey's curtains are closed. I'm dying to know what's going on over there.

A bolt of an idea practically knocks me off my feet. What if I go to Hailey Chun's party to get my special ingredient? I'd get a peek at the Haileys' secret world.

"Me!" I blurt. "I'm going first!"

Elbow Macaroni

It's three forty-five. I call Mom and ask her if it's okay for us to walk around the neighborhood. She says it's fine as long as we stay together. Since I'm not allowed to have a cell phone until I turn thirteen, Mom gets Todd's number and Manga Girl's number, just in case. Then I write a note for Tutu and slide it under her bedroom door.

> We went to get stuff for the sleepover soup. Back soon.

She can't be mad. The soup was her idea!

"Where are we going?" Todd asks.

"You'll see." I turn off the stove, then grab my raincoat

from the closet. Autumn gets hers. William is still wearing his plaid coat, and Manga Girl has her cape. Todd insists he doesn't need a coat, even though he's wearing shorts.

"We need something to carry our ingredients," Todd says as he dumps all the stuff out of his backpack—toothbrush, pajamas, an extra pair of underwear. I cringe. Todd's tighty-whities are lying on my living room floor! He slings the empty pack over his shoulder. "Okay, I'm good to go."

I double-check to make sure I have my apartment key and bus pass. While we wait for the elevator, Manga Girl reaches out and touches William's hat. "I'm glad it's fake," she says. "I don't like people who wear real fur." I'm not about to tell her that Tutu has an old mink coat in the back of her closet. It has moth holes in it. I've tried it on, and it smells pretty bad, the way an old dog smells. She never wears it.

When we crowd into the elevator, Manga Girl takes the corner, as usual. Todd takes the center, Autumn and I on either side. William is the last to step in. During the ride, I start to worry a bit. I'm going to tell the Haileys that I've stopped by because I'm on a scavenger hunt and it's part of this amazing sleepover I'm hosting. Hopefully, they'll be impressed and they'll want to come to my next sleepover. But what if they see Todd, Manga Girl, and William? They'll think we're all friends. Because that's what a normal person does, right? A normal person invites her *friends* to a sleepover.

Once we're in the lobby, I lead everyone past the ugly plastic plant. A spider has spun its web between the plant and the wall. Because I'm about to go to a new, modern building, I become painfully aware of our chipped floor tiles, the fading paint, and the stacks of junk mail. To makes things worse, the radiator is filling the lobby with hot, stuffy air. It's such a relief to step outside. The world smells damp, and a breeze cools my face. The pavement is glossy wet. It's not pouring, just sprinkling enough that car wipers swish as they pass by. Manga Girl tucks her sketchbook beneath her cape.

"You guys wait here," I tell them when we get to Hailey's building. We stand under the awning.

"What? Why?" Todd asks.

"Because I'm going upstairs to Hailey Chun's apartment." I want Hailey to myself. This is my moment. "I'll be right back."

"Hailey Chun lives here?" Manga Girl cringes. "She's so stuck-up."

Wait. What? Someone's insulting one of the Haileys? "She's not stuck-up," I say.

Manga Girl looks me right in the eye. "Yes, she is. And she's mean."

"Mean?" Maybe Manga Girl's jealous of Hailey, since Hailey has so many friends. "You don't know what you're saying. Hailey Chun isn't mean."

"I know *exactly* what I'm saying. She always talks about people behind their backs." A strand of Manga Girl's curly black hair pops out from under her hat. She tucks it back into place. "Why would you want to be friends with someone like that?"

For a moment, I'm not sure what to say. I've been sitting next to the big round table all year, and I've never heard Hailey Chun talk about other people in a mean way. Well, maybe she does *sometimes* talk about other people, but it's only because she has very specific taste in clothing and most of the kids at school don't dress as trendy as she does. But those kids *never* know she's talking about them, so that doesn't really count as being mean. "Who are you to call someone mean, after you drew that cartoon of me?" I point out.

"It's not done—I already told you that."

"Hey, are we going to stand out here in the rain arguing about stupid stuff, or are we going on a scavenger hunt?" Todd asks.

I take a deep breath. Manga Girl's really getting

under my skin. "I think Hailey Chun is great. She's a good friend of mine, and I'm going to get my sleepover soup ingredient from her." Autumn bites her lower lip. Of course, she knows the truth. Hailey Chun isn't my good friend, but that lie shot out of my mouth before I could think about it, and it's too late to take it back.

The doorman opens the door for us. He's a really tall guy with a long, skinny neck and an Adam's apple that's so big it looks like he swallowed something and it got stuck in his throat. I wonder if he likes wearing the uniform. It has those things on the shoulders, like a pilot's jacket. "May I help you?" he asks. His name tag reads BILL.

"Hi, Bill," I say. I've never been in Hailey Chun's lobby. The floor is polished marble, the paint is a warm buttery color, and there are no fake, dust-covered plants. "We're here to see Hailey." I pull on Autumn's sleeve until she stands next to me. "Hailey Chun."

"Are you here for the sleepover?" Bill asks.

"Not *exactly*," I say. "I'm having my own sleepover. But I need to ask Hailey a question. We go to the same school. I live right across the street." I point.

"Yeah, I know. I've seen you." He taps his foot. "The thing is, she's got guests right now."

"Autumn and I just want to get a piece of homework

from her." Another lie. But at least that one sounded believable. "They'll wait here." I tip my head toward Todd, Manga Girl, and William. Todd frowns. Manga Girl sits in a lobby chair. William pulls his hat over his eyes.

"Well, seeing as you go to school with Hailey, I think it's okay to send you up." Bill motions us toward the elevator.

Autumn hesitates. "I don't really want to—"

"I need you," I whisper to her. "So Hailey will know that I'm actually having a party."

"It's apartment six B," Bill tells us. He reaches into the elevator and presses button number six.

"Okay," I say. "Thanks." A little shiver runs across my shoulders. Apartment 6B is the same number as my apartment. That has to be a sign that Hailey and I are meant to be friends. "We'll be right back," I call out to the others.

When the elevator doors close, Autumn and I are finally alone. I clench my fists. "Manga Girl makes me so mad. She wonders why I want to be friends with someone like Hailey Chun. Can you believe that?"

Autumn doesn't say anything. She doesn't need to. I know she agrees with me. We agree on most everything, except for that whole thing about keeping food items from touching. That doesn't bother me at all.

The elevator rises. Second floor. Third floor. This is the chance I've longed for—the chance to see inside a Hailey party. It feels like going to a secret clubhouse. My whole body starts tingling.

"What are you going to borrow?" Autumn whispers when we step out.

"I don't know," I say. I stop in my tracks. "What do you think I should borrow?"

"Something that's delicious in chicken broth?"

I nod. That sounds like a good plan.

As I stand in front of 6B, I realize my hands are shaking. Autumn stands behind me, trying to hide. That's pretty easy, since she's about half my size. I take another deep breath, then ring the doorbell. The door opens right away. It's Mrs. Chun.

"Hello?" she says with surprise.

"Uh, hi. I'm Leilani." My voice sounds squeaky all of a sudden. "I . . . I live across the street. Hailey and I are in the same class."

"Hello, Leilani. Yes, I remember you. I'm afraid Hailey is busy with guests right now." She speaks with a slight accent and wears bright red lipstick. "Maybe you could wait and talk to her at school on Monday?"

"Well . . . the thing is . . ." If I tell Mrs. Chun that I need an ingredient for soup, she might get it for me, and then I won't see Hailey. I decide it's best to keep lying. "I wanted to ask her about some homework."

"Homework?" Mrs. Chun nods. "Very well. I'll go get her." She disappears.

I take a step and lean into the entryway. There's a coat closet and a rack for shoes. Six pairs of purple Converse are lined up. Apparently, the Haileys bought the exact same shoes, then personalized them with markers. One pair has flowers, another has butterflies. The pair I like best is covered in happy faces. My gaze travels up the wall, to a row of family photos. The Chuns are posed in front of a ski lodge. In another photo, Hailey and her little brother are on a beach holding surfboards. I take another half step, and though I can see down the hall, I can't see into the living room. It's pretty quiet in there. I expected lots of dance music and crazy laughter. What's going on? What's the theme? Are they playing a game of Truth or Dare? Whispering secrets?

Footsteps creak behind me. I turn around. Todd, Manga Girl, and William took the stairs and are now standing in the hallway.

"What are you doing up here?" I ask. "I thought you were gonna wait in the lobby." Sure, I want Hailey to know I'm having a party, but her seeing my actual guests could ruin everything.

"Todd insisted," Manga Girl says. Then she sits on the floor and starts drawing. William stays by the stairwell. But Todd strides right up to us.

"Look, Leilani, this is a group game," he says. "It's not fair to take only one player with you."

"Player?" I quickly check over my shoulder, to make sure Hailey isn't coming. Then I lower my voice. "Todd, this isn't a basketball game. It's a scavenger hunt for a made-up recipe. I don't see a problem with taking only one person."

"But the recipe said we have to do this *together* or it won't work. We have to do this as a team." He smiles at Autumn. She makes a weird face, like she's going to burp or something.

I'm pretty sure Todd is making up these rules, but I can't quite remember. I groan. What he doesn't seem to realize is that the recipe isn't going to work no matter what happens. It's just one of Tutu's crazy stories. Why doesn't Todd get that? No moon goddess, no magic. We'll probably all get diarrhea from the soup.

"Listen, Todd, I want to do this by myself. I—"

"Hi, Leilani."

I spin back around. Hailey Chun stands in her entryway. I swallow hard. "Uh, hi, Hailey."

"Mom said you wanted something." Her upper lip curls. "Well?" She sounds annoyed, the same way I sounded when Mom forced me to have this sleepover. "What do you want?"

I can't remember. All I know, at this moment, is that Hailey is holding a plastic cup. A paper umbrella with a skewered maraschino cherry and a pineapple wedge sticks out the top. That's the kind of drink I was going to make for my party. And she's wearing a bright orange plastic lei. Is she having a Hawaiian luau? But that was my theme!

Autumn pokes me in the back. "Borrow something," she whispers.

"Oh right." I clear my throat. "I'm wondering if I could borrow—"

"What are *they* doing here?" Hailey looks past my shoulder.

I try to block Hailey's view, but Todd's so tall, it's like trying to block a tree. "So anyway, I was wondering if—"

"Hi, Hailey." Todd leans against the doorframe. "How's it going?"

Hailey smiles at him. "Hi, Todd. What are you doing?" *Wait a minute.* Are Hailey and Todd friends?

"I'm with Leilani. She invited me to a sleepover. We're on a scavenger hunt."

Hailey's lip curls again. "*You're* hanging out with Leilani?"

"Sure," he says. Is he going to tell her we're cousins? I always try to avoid that subject, but if Hailey and Todd are friends, then maybe, on this one occasion, it won't be such a bad thing to admit.

Mrs. Chun's voice calls out that the shredded pork sandwiches are ready. Todd straightens. "Hey, Hailey. Can I get a sandwich? Leilani forgot to get food for the sleepover, and I'm starving."

I could have punched him. Now Hailey will think I'm a terrible host who doesn't feed her guests. Todd is *ruining* everything. "I didn't forget," I mumble. "I just . . . I just . . ."

"I didn't know *you* had sleepovers," Hailey says.

I brighten up. "Of course I have sleepovers. I have them all the time. They're the best. We always have so much fun, don't we?" I reach back and tap Autumn on the arm.

"Yes," Autumn says quietly. She's still hiding behind me.

"Wait. You do sleepovers *all the time*?" Todd frowns at me. "How come you've never invited me until now?"

"Because . . ." Jeez, this conversation is not going in the direction I hoped. Would Hailey ask why I hadn't invited her?

"It's a Hawaiian luau sleepover," Manga Girl announces, real loud, from her place on the floor. "At least, that's what it said on the invite."

Hailey gasps. "You stole my idea?"

"No, of course I didn't steal your idea." I feel my face heat up. How can she think such a thing? "I love Hawaiian food. I'm half Hawaiian, remember?" She doesn't look convinced. In fact, she looks even more annoyed. And she's not listening to me. She's staring at William, who's pacing at the end of the hall. His coat is so big it makes him look like a little kid who's borrowed his dad's coat. A lump forms in my throat. Maybe it *is* his dad's coat. I remember the cruddy thing we have in common. But I don't have time to feel sad right now, because my moment with Hailey is veering off the runway. "If you'd like to do a scavenger hunt with me, I can have another sleepover next weekend and invite you."

Hailey's still staring. "Who *is* that?" she asks.

"That's a new kid. He doesn't go to our school." I try to get her attention by speaking louder. "Anyway, like I said, I'm doing this amazing scavenger hunt and

I need . . ." Something simple. Something everyone has. Something that tastes good in chicken broth. "A box of pasta!"

"Why are you yelling?" She rolls her eyes. "Whatever. Wait here." And off she goes.

"Don't forget a sandwich," Todd calls.

"I wasn't *yelling*," I mumble. I look at Autumn for support, and she squeezes my hand.

We wait in the hallway. William keeps pacing. Manga Girl keeps drawing. Todd's practically drooling. Hailey didn't invite me into her secret clubhouse. She made me stay in the hall. Maybe I should have followed her?

"Hi, Leilani." Hayley Ranson appears. She's wearing a yellow lei and carrying one of those umbrella drinks. "I heard you're having a scavenger hunt? That sounds like fun. We're just watching a movie." She sighs. "I wish I could—"

"You wish you could what?" Hailey Chun's back. She scowls at Hayley. "How come you're talking to *her*?" Hayley dashes away.

Why did Hailey say the word *her* in that way? As if it tasted bad?

Hailey hands me a box of pasta. Elbow macaroni.

"Thanks," I say. This is it. My opportunity. It's now or never. "So the next time I have a sleepover I'll invite you and the rest of the Haileys." I smile hopefully. "Would you like that?"

"Thanks, but no thanks." She closes the door in my face.

"Awkward," Todd says.

A few minutes of uncomfortable silence pass, but it feels like a million years. Then we all cram into the elevator. Everyone's looking at me, even William. "I thought you and Hailey Chun were friends," Manga Girl says.

I shoot her a super-icy look. "We are," I insist.

"Well, if it makes you feel any better, she forgot to get me a sandwich." Todd takes the box of macaroni and sticks it into his backpack. It doesn't make me feel better. Hailey hadn't sneered at Todd. She hadn't accused him of stealing her party theme. And she hadn't shut the door in his face.

"Okay, I'm next!" he announces when we reach the lobby.

And just like that the scavenger hunt is a real thing, and we are following Todd down the sidewalk.

It's still sprinkling, but each raindrop feels as heavy

as a brick. Kāne and Lono and those other gods could unleash a hurricane, but it wouldn't make me feel any worse. Because this afternoon I learned something that I wish I never learned.

Hailey Chun doesn't like me.

Basketball Dreams

I don't know where Todd is taking us, and I don't care. I just want to go home and erase this day from my memory. Autumn walks next to me, but she doesn't say anything. She doesn't need to ask me a bunch of questions, because she knows how I'm feeling. That's how it is with best friends.

I go over the scene in my head. There were warning signs—the eye roll, the sneer, the tone of her voice. But I ignored them. I went right ahead and asked her if she wanted to come to my next sleepover. The final blow was the door slamming in my face.

There has to be an explanation. Did Hailey judge me because of my guests, just as I feared she would? That makes sense. But then I remember that she smiled at Todd, so she clearly likes him. That's a point in my favor.

And she doesn't know anything about William, so that's not a point against me. But what about Manga Girl? Manga Girl doesn't like Hailey. She called her mean. If the feeling is mutual and Hailey doesn't like Manga Girl, and now Hailey thinks that Manga Girl and I are friends . . . is that the problem?

But as much as I try to convince myself that this is Manga Girl's fault, I can't forget the moment when Hailey first came to the door. When Hailey looked at me, she sneered. And that was long before she noticed Manga Girl.

It's me. She doesn't like *me*.

"Four more blocks," Todd says.

"I don't want to do this anymore," I tell him.

He jumps over a puddle. "We can't quit, Leilani. You got your ingredient. Now it's my turn. Wait till you see my special place. It's awesome."

There are puddles everywhere, and I almost step in dog poop that the rain turned to paste. An ambulance races past, its siren blaring. "Why are we going toward Pill Hill?" I ask. It's called Pill Hill because it's a hill with a bunch of hospitals on it.

Todd turns around and smiles. "You'll see."

I don't care if I'm supposed to have a good attitude about my sleepover. I'm walking the slowest because

I can't stop thinking about what just happened. *Devastated* is not a strong enough word. Even if, at that moment, Hailey Chun is the only Hailey who doesn't like me, I know it's only a matter of time before she persuades the others to dislike me, too. I picture a line of toppling dominoes, with the faces of all the Haileys taped to them.

Autumn stays next to me. William walks in the middle, and Manga Girl walks super fast to keep up with Todd, whose legs are three times as long as ours. No matter what I look at—the sidewalk, the buildings, the back of William's fur hat—all I can see is the expression on Hailey's face, just before she shut the door. She looked like she ate a lemon.

I bump into William, who has stopped walking. So have Todd and Manga Girl. "Ta-da," Todd says, sweeping his arms. He stands next to a stone wall. A big red sign is mounted on the wall: THE UNIVERSITY OF SEATTLE.

"What's so special about this place?" Manga Girl asks.

Todd leans against the stones. "My dad and my mom went to college here. They both played basketball. Dad was the center and Mom was center forward. This is where they want me to go. I'm gonna be an Otter."

Manga Girl's ears twitch. "An otter?"

"It's the mascot." He points to a student who's walking past. Her red sweatshirt reads: U OF S OTTERS. "Yep, this is where I'm gonna go."

I shove my hands into my raincoat pockets. "We're only in sixth grade, Todd. College is a long time from now. You never know what might happen."

"What do you mean?" he asks.

I'm feeling sour, as sour as Hailey's expression. "There are lots of basketball players out there who might be better than you. Or you could get injured. You might not get in." I'm being snotty. Everything feels wrong.

Mom would say, *Leilani, don't use that tone with me*, and Tutu would say, *Watch your toes and fingers—she's snapping like a sea turtle.*

"Yeah, I might not get in." Todd frowns and rubs the back of his neck. "All I know is that it's really important to my parents that I play basketball here. This is where they met. I wouldn't have been born if it hadn't been for basketball and this school."

"Forget college," Manga Girl tells him. "I'm going to New York, and I'm going to live in a loft and make graphic novels." William doesn't add anything to the conversation. But he's listening.

Autumn starts to raise her hand but stops herself. "I just read an article about university admission," she says.

"Really?" Todd asks. "You read stuff like that?"

"Well, I know that I want to go to college. So I've been preparing. Admission to a university is more competitive than ever. You need a high GPA and excellent SAT scores, AP classes, teacher recommendations, and—" She pauses. Todd's frown has turned into a grimace. "But I'm sure you'll get in because you're a good athlete. I bet you'll get a scholarship."

Todd doesn't say anything. Why does he look so worried? It doesn't surprise me that Autumn's been thinking about college. But Todd is thinking about it, too. Do we already have to start planning our futures? That seems crazy.

"So?" Manga Girl asks. "Is this your special place? This wall?"

"No. It's across campus."

Lots of students are walking around. Because of his height, Todd is the only one in our group who looks like he might be old enough to go to college. But nobody stops us and asks us why we're on campus. The color red is everywhere—on signs, buildings—and most people we pass are wearing red shirts. We cross a street, then follow Todd up some stairs and into the University of Seattle's athletic center.

The lobby is lined with trophy cases and some big, framed photos of teams. A group of cheerleaders sits at a corner table, holding a meeting. The girls wear red skirts, the boys red shorts. With her red cape, Manga Girl fits right in. Todd leads us through some double doors, into a huge basketball arena. The wooden floor is shiny, with a red border around it. The word OTTERS is painted on the floor under one of the hoops. There must have been a game recently because the place is littered with water bottles, candy wrappers, and popcorn containers.

"Wow," Todd says. "I've been here to see games, but I've never been here when it's empty. This is so cool." He grabs a ball from a cart and runs onto the court. Then he shoots a basket and, just like that, the ball goes into the hoop. I figure he's going to do this for a while, so I sit on a bleacher. Autumn sits next to me. Manga Girl climbs way up to the top bleacher, takes out her sketch-book, and starts drawing. William sits by himself, in the middle section, watching from under the rim of his fur hat as Todd runs around, dribbling the ball, making every single shot.

"Why do you think Hailey Chun doesn't like me?" I whisper to Autumn.

"I don't think she *doesn't* like you," Autumn says.

"Didn't you see the way she looked at me before she slammed the door in my face?" I try to keep my voice low, but the words want to burst out. "She *glared* at me."

"I think . . ." Autumn wraps an arm around my shoulder and gives me a half hug. "I think she was focused on her party and her guests. We were an inconvenient interruption. That's all."

As I think this over, I let out a slow breath. Yes, that makes sense. Hailey was rude because she was stressed out. Hosting a sleepover is a lot of work. If my sleepover invitations hadn't gotten mixed up and mailed to the wrong people, I would have worked real hard on the food and the games, and making sure the apartment was clean. I would have borrowed one of Tutu's sundresses and put flowers in my hair. I would have played music by our favorite Hawaiian singer—Iz Kamakawiwo'ole.

"But she said no thanks when I invited her to my next sleepover," I point out.

Autumn hesitates. Then she says, "I think your timing was bad."

"Yeah, bad timing." I want to feel better, but I'm still prickly. My single-minded goal has been to become one of the Haileys. How can I make that happen if Hailey Chun wants nothing to do with me? "Is Todd done yet?" I grumble.

The arena goes quiet all of a sudden. Todd's sitting on one of the front benches, his head hanging, his shoulders hunched. What's he doing? His shoulders start to shake. Wait, is Todd crying? Autumn looks at me. She mouths, *What should we do?* I mouth, *I don't know.* It would be really awkward if we went down there. Wouldn't it?

"Whoosh." A shape rushes by. Manga Girl, who doesn't seem to care about being awkward, runs down the stairs, her cape flying behind her. She plops herself on the bench next to Todd. "Are you crying?" she asks.

"No." Todd quickly wipes his face with his hand. "I'm *not* crying."

So he *is* crying. *Yikes!* Autumn and I bolt to our feet, then hurry down the aisle. William stays where he is, but he's watching. "What's wrong?" I ask Todd.

He wedges the basketball between his feet. "I won't get in," he says. Even though he's stopped crying, his eyes still glisten. "I'll never get accepted here. They'll never take me. Leilani's right." He leans forward, his arms resting on his knees, and hangs his head.

Manga Girl scowls at me. "That wasn't a nice thing to say."

"Hey, wait a minute." I shuffle in place. "I didn't say Todd *wouldn't* get in. I said he *might not* get in. That's totally different." Todd sniffles. Is he going to start crying again? I don't want him to cry. I didn't mean to get him all upset. "Look," I tell him, trying to fix things. "You're the tallest kid in school, so you got that going for you. And you make every single basket."

"You're our school's star player," Autumn adds softly.

"Star player?" Todd wipes his face again, then looks up. "Have you guys ever been to one of my games?" Autumn, Manga Girl, and I shake our heads. We aren't exactly the sporty types. Todd shrugs. "If you haven't been to one of the games, then you don't know the truth."

The truth?

Is Todd hiding some kind of secret?

Go, Todd, Go

I've never been to one of Todd's basketball games. Actually, I've never been to any basketball games. I've never even watched one on TV. Thanks to Ms. Delridge, the physical education teacher at our school, I basically know how the game works. She makes us play it a few times a year, but I really hate all that running around, and all the pushing and elbowing. And tripping, and foot-stomping. It's like a war zone out there. Liza Zurlinden, a girl in our school, doesn't have to take PE because she's pigeon-toed. I have to take PE, even though I'm more of a klutz than Liza. Being pigeon-toed is an actual medical condition, but being a klutz isn't. I know because Autumn looked it up.

"What do you mean, we don't know the truth?" I ask Todd.

"Are you hiding something?" Manga Girl lifts her cape so it covers the lower half of her face. "Do you have a *secret identity*?"

"It's not a secret." Todd kicks the basketball real hard. It flies across the court. "The truth is . . . I'm a benchwarmer."

Manga Girl drops her cape. Autumn's mouth falls open. I scrunch up my face. "Huh?"

He groans. "I don't play in the games. I sit on the bench."

"What are you talking about?" I ask. "If you don't play, then why do you wear your uniform all the time?"

"Coach hasn't kicked me off the team because I'm good in practice. You saw me, right? I make every basket." Autumn, Manga Girl, and I nod. William sits very still, listening from the middle section of the bleachers. Todd grips the edge of the bench. "But during a game I get . . ." He lets go of the bench and clenches his fists. "I freak out, okay? I go out there, in front of a crowd, and I feel weird. I can't focus. I get dizzy. I get confused. I get . . ." He grimaces. "I get mental or something."

No one says anything. Todd is clenching his fists so hard his knuckles turn white.

"You're not mental," Autumn says calmly. Her raincoat makes crinkling sounds as she sits next to him.

"You just get scared. That's all." Boy, if anyone understands getting scared in front of an audience, it's Autumn. She always turns red, and her hands start shaking. Last week she gave an oral report on Chief Sealth for our Washington state history unit, and just before it was her turn, she told me she felt like she was going to throw up. "If I have to do anything in front of an audience, I get the same symptoms—dizziness, confusion, inability to focus. It's called stage fright."

He looks at her, waiting for more. We all look at her.

"Stage fright is a sort of general anxiety." Autumn nervously fiddles with the zipper on her coat. "When I stand in front of an audience, I worry that some embarrassing event might occur. That I'll trip and fall. Forget my lines. Make a huge mistake." She swallows hard. "Get laughed at."

Todd's hands relax. "Yeah, I guess that's it. What if something bad happens?"

Mom said that Todd was having a hard time. Was this what she was talking about? "Why are you worried about something bad happening?" I ask. "You've got perfect aim."

"Yeah, my aim's good, but . . ." He bolts to his feet. "It's a lot of pressure." He starts pacing. "My parents were the best. The *best*. They *lived* basketball. All they ever talk about is the glory years when they won all those trophies. But what if I go out there and . . ." Autumn blinks her big eyes at him. "What if I miss? What if we lose the game because I mess up? Those thoughts go round and round in my head, and my legs get wobbly and my hands get sweaty. I can't get a good grip on the ball." He stops pacing. "The thing is, I really like basketball. It's the only thing I'm good at. But this year I don't know what happened. During the first game, I kind of lost it. I couldn't make a single basket. So I've been benched the whole season." His voice grows louder. "What if I can't ever get over this? What if I'm like this for the rest of my life?" That question echoes off the arena walls.

I pretend I need to find something in my pocket, but, really, I'm embarrassed. We've seen Todd crying, and now he's telling us his biggest fear. The truth is, I don't know him very well. Sure, I've spent Thanksgivings at his house, where he tortured me by eating whipped cream with his pumpkin pie, then aiming deadly farts at me. But I never really talked to him. And here he is, admitting some deep, personal stuff. I thought he was our star basketball player, but it turns out he's too scared to play.

Too scared to play.

I don't know what to say to him. I feel even worse that I made those comments about him not getting into college, but now I realize that what I said might very well be the truth!

The sound of footsteps breaks the silence. William's running toward the exit. There's no use asking him where he's going. Maybe he needs to use the bathroom. Or maybe he's bored and he's going home. He and his big plaid coat disappear through the doorway. We're not supposed to walk around the city alone, so I'm about to call out to him, when I realize that he hasn't gone anywhere. He simply slipped behind the door. "He's gonna whisper something," I realize. We all go quiet so we can hear.

"Whisper, whisper."

"What's that?" I holler. "Can you say it again?"

"Whisper, whisper."

"Dude, we can't hear you," Todd calls.

"He said, 'exposure therapy,'" Manga Girl tells us. I look at her with surprise. She shrugs and points to her fox ears. "I have superior hearing." William walks back inside, takes his seat in the middle section, folds his hands in his lap, and just sits there.

I thought William couldn't get any weirder, but he just proved me wrong. "What's he talking about?"

"I know," Autumn says. She turns on the bench and

looks up at William. "Exposure therapy is a type of behavioral therapy. The theory is that if you expose yourself to your fear, over and over, you'll begin to feel a sense of control, and the fear will eventually go away." William nods.

Manga Girl chews on the end of her pencil. "They did something like that in Critter League issue number sixty-seven."

"Is that one of your comic books?" I ask.

She folds her arms and glares at me. "Critter League is not a *comic book*, Leilani. It's manga. Manga is an art form."

"What did they do in issue sixty-seven?" Autumn asks. I can't believe she's interested. She doesn't like those kinds of stories. I plop onto the bench next to her.

Manga Girl pushes her cape behind her shoulders. "Well, global warming melted the northern ice cap, exposing the league's headquarters, so they had to rebuild in a new secret location. So in issue sixty-seven, Beaverboy, who's the leader, chose a tiny island in the middle of Lake Forgotten. But the Toxic Riders were on alert, flying over the area, so he told his team that, instead of using a boat, they must swim to and from the island to avoid detection. Lynxgirl was too afraid of water to cross, because she's part feline. On the first day, she stood next to the water. On the second day, she stuck her foot in. On the third day, she waded in up to her knees. On the fourth day, she agreed to float. On the fifth day, she put her face in the water. On the sixth day, she tried swimming, and on the seventh day, she swam to headquarters and was never afraid of the water again." Manga Girl frowns. "Only problem was, because she spent all that time dealing with her fear, she missed out on some crucial intelligence briefings regarding the Garbage Island Mission, and she didn't get a major storyline again until issue seventy-two."

Longest. Explanation. Ever.

Todd rubs his ear. "What's that got to do with *my* problem?"

"Lynxgirl used exposure therapy," Autumn tells him. "She slowly exposed herself to the water and, thus, conquered her fear. I think William mentioned it because, well, because I think he wants you to try it. Is that right, William?" He nods.

Todd still doesn't get it. And I don't get it, either. But Autumn does. She gets everything. She scurries onto the court and grabs a basketball. Then she comes back and hands it to Todd. "You're worried about making mistakes in front of a crowd, right?"

"Uh-huh."

"Then go shoot baskets. We'll be your spectators. We'll make all sorts of noise, just like a real audience."

Manga Girl leaps onto the bench. "Yeah, we'll scream and stomp and try to distract you."

"But you're not a real crowd," Todd tells her. "This isn't a real game. I don't feel nervous."

Autumn chews on her lower lip. She looks toward the exit. She looks at Todd. Then she holds up a finger. "Wait here." Faster than I've ever seen her move, she races out of the arena. Where is she going? I don't see how this therapy thing could possibly work. Like Todd said, he doesn't feel nervous around us. And besides, it took Lynxgirl a whole week to swim to the island, and we need to get back to the apartment before dark.

"Where is he?"

"Is that him?"

"Hey, kid! You think you can shoot? Show us what you got!"

The cheer squad hurries into the arena. There are fifteen of them, and they spread out along the red border and begin stomping and cheering. Some wave pom-poms. One of the guys does a backflip. "T! O! Double D! T! O! Double D!" Todd stands like a statue as they cheer his name. I'm equally shocked. *What. Is. Going. On?*

Autumn hurries back to our bench, a big grin on her face. "Autumn, what did you do?" I ask.

She's out of breath, and her cheeks are red. "I told them that Todd is a really good basketball player, but that the coach benched him because he has stage fright. I told them that he needs to practice in front of a crowd." She gasps for air. "I think this might help."

I can't believe it. Autumn talked to a bunch of strangers? That's a really big deal!

Todd hurries over. "What's going on?" he asks us. "Why are all these cheerleaders shouting my name?"

"Go, Todd, go!"

"Don't look at me," I say, my hands in the air. "This wasn't my idea."

Autumn is still breathing pretty hard. Apparently, she needs to get more exercise. Too much time with books, probably. "This is your exposure therapy," she tells him. "You can practice with a crowd. They'll be your crowd."

"No way," he says, shaking his head. Then he scowls at her. "I'm not doing it!"

"But I thought . . ." She frowns. "I'm sorry. I didn't mean to butt in." She slowly sits on the bench. Her shoulders slump.

"Jeez, Todd, you didn't have to yell at her. She was only trying to help," I tell him.

The same guy does a backflip again. "Go, Todd, go!"

Todd shuffles in place. "Sorry, Autumn. I didn't mean to yell at you. I'm just . . ." He looks around. "I don't think this will work."

Suddenly, William's standing next to Todd. Even his walking is silent. He hands Todd a basketball. Todd grimaces as he clutches the ball. Manga Girl starts jumping up and down. "Go, Todd, go!" she shouts. William starts stomping his feet. Because all the noises are echoing, it sounds like the crowd has tripled in size.

Todd looks down at Autumn. I know by the way her head is hanging that she's trying to disappear into her raincoat. That was a super brave thing she did, going out there and talking to the cheerleaders. He doesn't understand how shy she is. So I start to feel really mad at Todd for hurting her feelings. And I'm about to tell him that when he wanders onto the court. He moves like he's in a slow-motion dream. He wipes his palms on his shorts. Then he stands in front of the hoop. He dribbles the ball a few times, looks around. The cheerleaders jump up and down. Seriously, why is this such a big deal? I just saw him shoot dozens of baskets. He can do this.

But his hands are shaking. And his face has gone really pale. I want to close my eyes, because I know what's about to happen, like a sign on the freeway that flashes ACCIDENT AHEAD. And won't that be extra embarrassing for him? To miss in front of everyone? But I can't look away. Even Autumn looks up.

Todd takes aim.

The ball leaves his hand and flies through the air.

And misses the basket.

As the ball rolls away, everyone falls into silence. Todd doesn't move. But William walks across the court, picks up the ball, and throws it back to Todd. The cheer squad starts hollering again. "Basket! Basket!"

Todd wipes his forehead. He dribbles again. He looks around. Dribbles. Takes aim.

Another miss.

We all groan. This is painful. That toss was at least a foot off. He's worse than me!

Again, William collects the ball and throws it to Todd. Todd looks over at Autumn. The cheer squad starts again. I'm starting to feel really bad for Todd. How long is he going to do this? Maybe it would be best to stop him? To save him from feeling like a failure. Maybe I could yell something like, *It's getting late! We need to get going!* But he's standing in front of the hoop again.

He aims, shoots, and . . .

The ball goes right through. A shiver darts up my spine. "Woo-hoo!" I cry. Everyone goes nuts. Even Autumn.

Todd begins to move, dribbling here, dribbling there. He shoots again and it goes in. And again. After the tenth basket, I take a break. I mean, I can only cheer for so long before my throat starts to burn. After the twelfth basket, everyone stops. Todd gets some pats on the back and a couple of handshakes, and the cheer squad leaves. When Todd runs over to us, his face is sweaty, his eyes on fire. "That was the best," he says. "I did it!" Then he puts a hand on Autumn's shoulder. "Thanks, Autumn."

Wow, I've never seen Autumn's face turn that red. Chili pepper red! "It was William's idea," she says, looking away.

"Hey, William," Todd calls. "How did you know about . . . what did you call it?"

"Exposure therapy," Autumn says.

"Yeah, how'd you know about exposure therapy?"

William doesn't say anything. Todd sets the basketball

back on the cart. "He probably learned about it from a psychiatrist," I whisper to Autumn. She nods. Then I wonder if coming to my sleepover is part of William's exposure therapy. That's an interesting twist. My mixed-up sleepover might actually help someone get better?

"Once my hands stopped shaking, I was okay out there," Todd says. "I'm gonna tell Coach about this. I'm going to tell him how I've been feeling. I mean, I know I'm not cured, but if I tell Coach, then maybe he'll put me into the game just a few minutes at a time. Or maybe he'll let me practice in front of a crowd. Will you guys help me?"

"Sure," Manga Girl says. Autumn nods.

"How 'bout you, cuz?"

"Yeah, okay." I imagine Autumn and me dressed like cheerleaders. Manga Girl, too, only her outfit has a cape. As I'm wondering if William would want to join our squad, a ball comes flying at my face.

"Think fast!"

I grab the ball that Todd's thrown at me. I'm not sure what I'm doing—I think it's called traveling—but I'm heading for the basket. Everyone's on the court now, even William. We play a really terrible game, probably the worst game ever played in the history of basketball. Todd's laughing, but not in a mean way. Autumn's so short her ball doesn't even get close to the net. So before she can protest, Todd scoops her onto his shoulders and charges. She scores!

"Hey, you kids!" A janitor walks in, pushing a trash can on wheels. "You're not supposed to be in here. Get out before I call security."

"Sorry," I call as we scramble toward the exit. We're all smiling, even William. Did we just have fun? Manga Girl grabs her sketchbook, then *whoosh*es past me, leading the way.

"Wait, I forgot my ingredient," Todd says. He looks around. Then he grabs a half-eaten box of popcorn.

We are back outside. We escaped the grumpy janitor. The excitement of the basketball game fades away. We stand on the steps. The concrete is wet, though the rain has stopped. William, who was so busy with the basketballs, is once again sullen and looking at his feet. Todd sticks the popcorn container into his backpack.

"Wait, you're really taking that? You can't put popcorn in soup," I tell him.

"Why not?" he asks. "It's just corn."

"Yeah, but it's *used* corn. Someone else was eating it."

Todd reaches into the backpack, grabs a few kernels, and shoves them into his mouth. He chews and swallows. Then his eyes bulge out, and he grabs his throat. "Ack!

I just ate *used* corn." He starts laughing. I don't flinch. If he wants to get poisoned, that's his business. But I'm not going to eat that stuff. "So, who's next?" he asks.

"I'll go next," Manga Girl says. And with a sweep of her cape, we're off.

Uncle Galaxy

We've got a break in the rain. Patches of sky peek out between gray clouds. According to Tutu, the clouds are the land of the Hawaiian gods. That never made much sense to me. Why would the gods live in the sky when Hawaii is supposedly so beautiful? I'd choose white sandy beaches and warm ocean water over rain-filled clouds any day, but I think most people in Seattle would say that.

It's just starting to get dark, but not quite dark enough for headlights. Tutu loves this time, between day and night. She often sings a song called "Hawaiian Twilight."

> *Sun is sinking in Hawaii*
> *Little birds are in their nests*

I wonder if Tutu is still sleeping, or if she read my note. Good thing I turned off the stove. This scavenger hunt is taking a lot longer than I expected.

Because we all have bus passes, we jump onto a 60. Then we get off on East John Street and Broadway. With a series of *whoosh*es, Manga Girl leads us down the road. The good thing is, nobody really seems shocked by a girl in a red cape *whoosh*ing down the street. Capitol Hill is filled with all sorts of odd characters. In just three blocks, we pass a bearded man wearing lipstick and a skirt, a girl walking a rabbit on a leash, and a group of musicians beating drumsticks on buckets.

We stop outside a store called Uncle Galaxy's Comics. I've seen this store, but I've never gone inside. I'm not into superheroes. I like stories about real people, with real problems. Come to think of it, my current situation would make a good story. "It's closed," I say, pointing to the sign.

Manga Girl knocks on the door. "My uncle owns the place, so he'll let us in." She knocks again.

"Uncle Galaxy is your *actual* uncle?" Todd asks. She nods.

The door is opened by a short, fat man in a Batman shirt. He's twisted and piled his dreadlocks on the top of his head in a big knot. Swirly tattoos run down his left arm, and he wears two little hoop earrings. "Hi, Uncle Galaxy," Manga Girl says.

"Hi, Tanisha. I closed early so I could do inventory. Come on in." He waves us inside.

It's a small shop, crowded from floor to ceiling with comics, board games, bobbleheads, superhero action figures, that kind of stuff. Like most of Seattle, the shop smells like coffee. But it also smells like BO, probably from Uncle Galaxy's armpit stains.

We stand in front of a glass counter where all the trading cards are displayed. Uncle Galaxy squeezes behind the counter. Then he holds up a drawing. "Look, Tanisha, I got it framed." It's a black-and-white drawing of a girl with a cape, a coffee cup in one hand and rain clouds in the other. The caption reads: *Super SeattleGirl.* "I'm so proud of you."

"Whoa, you drew that?" Todd asks.

Uncle Galaxy smiles. "She's had two cartoons published in the *Seattle Weekly.*"

I admit I'm impressed. I don't know anyone in the sixth grade who's been published. And who can draw like that.

Uncle Galaxy hangs the picture back on its hook, then sits on a stool. "So, are these your friends?" he asks.

"No, they're *not* my friends," Manga Girl answers.

Jeez, that's kind of rude, I think. But I don't feel insulted. She's only telling the truth. Sure, we just played basketball, but that doesn't mean we're going to start hanging out.

"*Not* your friends?" her uncle asks.

"We all got invited to the same sleepover. That's why we're together." She looks through the glass. "You got any new Critter League packs?"

"Next week." Uncle Galaxy scratches his big belly. "So, aren't you going to introduce me to these people who are *not* your friends?"

"Yeah, okay." Manga Girl points at me. "That's Leilani. She calls me Manga Girl behind my back." I gulp, then try to look innocent. "She's the one who's having the sleepover, but she didn't want to invite us. There was a mix-up with the invitations. We're on the 'DO NOT invite' list, and those got mailed instead of the 'DO invite' list."

I cringe. How can she possibly know about the lists? The only people who know are my mom, Tutu, and Autumn. Autumn would *never* tell anyone. And my mom and Tutu don't even know Manga Girl or her family, so they couldn't have told.

"What's she talking about?" Todd asks, scowling so hard at me it looks like he has to poop. "You didn't want to invite us?"

"No. I mean . . . yes. I mean . . ." My whole face heats up. I don't know what to say. Manga Girl is right—we aren't friends. So what does it matter if they know the truth? Manga Girl was honest with me—she told me she didn't want to come to my party. She said, in front of everyone, that we aren't friends. And after seeing that mean comic she drew, why should I protect *her* feelings? If she wants the truth, I'm happy to admit it. Todd would understand the "DO NOT invite" list because he and I have never really gotten along.

But William is a different matter. In his note, he thanked me for inviting him. According to my mom, he's never been invited to a sleepover before. There's no reason to hurt his feelings. "I don't know what she's talking about," I say.

"She wanted to invite the Haileys and not us," Manga Girl tells Todd. "I heard her talking about it." She points to her fox ears. "I told you, I have superior hearing."

Wait a minute! So that's what Manga Girl does when she sits in the corner? "Eavesdropping is rude," I say, folding my arms real tight. Of course, when I eavesdrop, it's for a good reason. I *need* to learn more about the Haileys.

The Haileys. I realize it's been a long time since I last thought about them. Guess I've been distracted or something.

"You shouldn't listen to private conversations," I add.

"But that's how I get my best material." She pats her sketchbook.

"Mixed-up invitations sounds like an intriguing start to a story," Uncle Galaxy says with a smile. "But what kind of story? Comedy? Tragedy? Heroic quest?" He looks at Autumn.

Autumn clears her throat. "We're on a scavenger hunt," she says quietly.

"Ah, then heroic quest it is." Uncle Galaxy grabs a pot of coffee and fills a Darth Vader mug. He takes a long sip, then sets the mug on the counter. "You have my undivided attention. Please continue with the introductions."

"That's Autumn," Manga Girl says. "She's smart *and* nice. At school, she does whatever Leilani does. She basically lives in Leilani's shadow."

"What?" I blurt. Is Manga Girl calling me bossy? I don't tell Autumn to follow me around, it's just what she does, because we're best friends. "Autumn doesn't . . ." I look to my right. Autumn happens to be standing next to me, in my shadow, but that's just a weird coincidence because we're under a light that's shaped like a planet and it throws a big shadow. Autumn blinks a few times, but she doesn't say anything.

"To be in the shadows suggests the power of invisibility," Uncle Galaxy tells us. "That can come in handy on a quest."

Wow, Uncle Galaxy and Manga Girl are clearly related.

"And that's Todd. He's Leilani's second cousin, though she never admits it because he's always teasing and embarrassing her. When he's not nervous, he's got perfect aim."

Uncle Galaxy fiddles with a leather strap that winds around his wrist. "Perfect aim, huh? Well, accuracy is certainly another worthy power."

"Oh, and he's also got a crush on Autumn," Manga Girl adds.

Wait! What?

Autumn takes a couple steps back and tries to hide behind a cutout of Doctor Who. Todd doesn't deny anything. He just shrugs.

Todd has a crush on Autumn? Of all the girls in school, why does he have to choose my best friend? Is he doing it just to bug me? Poor Autumn. On Monday, we'll need to figure out a nice way to let Todd know that this relationship isn't going to happen. We'll come up with a plan during lunch. But then I remember that Manga Girl will be eavesdropping, so we'll have to work out the plan after school. A letter might work. *Dear Todd, I don't feel the same way. . . .*

"What about you?" Uncle Galaxy turns toward William. "What's your superpower?"

William's still standing next to the door, hands in the pockets of his coat. His face looks extra pale against the dark fur of his hat. His eyes dart around. I wonder if he's going to bolt. Or find a door to hide behind. But he looks down at his feet.

"That's William," Manga Girl explains. "He doesn't talk much."

Uncle Galaxy's expression turns very serious. "Silence can be a mighty powerful force," he says. "I think the world could do with more of it."

"Well, from what I can tell, he'll only talk if he's standing behind a door," Manga Girl says.

"That's right," Todd agrees.

Uncle Galaxy taps his fingers on the counter. "You know, most superheroes have things they can't do or things that make them vulnerable. Without adversity or weakness, the hero can't be challenged. This is known as the supreme ordeal."

"I can't drink milk," Todd says.

Autumn peeks out from behind Doctor Who's elbow. "I can't talk in front of groups."

I can't get the Haileys to like me, I think, but I'm not going to admit that aloud. "I don't have a supreme ordeal."

Manga Girl arranges her cape. "The real Fox Girl can't outrun dogs."

"Wolverine can't defend himself against magnets," Todd says. Then he and Manga Girl start listing heroes and their weaknesses.

"Badger Girl gets claustrophobic if she tries to tunnel through the earth."

"Iron Man has a weak heart that has to be reenergized by his armor."

"Raccoon Girl is vulnerable to fleas."

Todd and Manga Girl seem to share a common interest. Maybe he'll change his mind and start crushing on her instead of on Autumn.

Todd points to a shelf above Uncle Galaxy's head. "And Captain America carries his indestructible shield, which protects him against basically everything."

At the mention of the shield, William looks up. Uncle Galaxy raises an eyebrow, noticing William's sudden interest. He pushes his coffee mug aside, then grabs the shield. It's round, with a big star in the middle, and made of plastic. It's about the size of a salad plate, something a little kid might use for a Halloween costume.

"Here it is, a perfect replica." He holds it out to William, who takes it and inspects it carefully.

"I've got an idea," Manga Girl says, her fox ears twitching again. "William, what if you had that shield? Then you wouldn't have to hide behind a door to talk. You could talk from behind the shield instead."

"That's an interesting suggestion." Uncle Galaxy rubs his chin. "In theory, the shield would be better than a door because even someone with X-ray vision couldn't see through it."

For a moment, I think Manga Girl has come up with a great idea. A magnificent idea. It makes perfect sense. William wants to hide behind something, and doors aren't always available. I mean, what if he's in the middle of a theater and the place catches fire and he needs to yell, *FIRE*? He'd have to find a door, and by then, it could be too late. But this way he can simply whip the shield out of his backpack.

But William sets the shield on the counter and steps away. He probably made the right decision. It's bad enough not talking in public, but imagine if he started walking around with a toy shield all the time.

Uncle Galaxy reaches into a drawer and pulls out some fun-size candy bars. "Well, Tanisha, whether these are your friends or not, it would appear you have the perfect crew for your scavenger hunt quest. You have a leader." He tosses a bar to me. I'm the leader? Yeah, I guess I am. "And a ragtag crew with the special powers of invisibility"—a bar to Autumn—"accuracy"—a bar to Todd—"eavesdropping"—a bar to Manga Girl—"and communication." He tosses the last bar to William. Communication? That makes no sense. "So, for what are you scavenging, and how may I help?"

"We're making sleepover soup," Todd says as he eats his Milky Way. I open my Snickers, which isn't my favorite, but I'm getting really hungry. I wish I had some of those Cheerios. "We each have to get an ingredient from a special place, then we put it in the soup."

"This is my special place," Manga Girl says.

Uncle Galaxy smiles. "Well, that does sound like an adventure." He glances at the clock. It's shaped like Saturn. "But duty calls. You kids are welcome to hang out as long as you'd like, but I've got to get back to work." He doesn't ask any more questions about the soup. Maybe a soup-making quest is an everyday sort of thing in a comic book store. "Oh, I almost forgot. That new Critter League hood you ordered came in." He hands Manga Girl a plastic bag. "Okay, I'll be in the storage room if you need me." He puts on a pair of headphones, grabs his coffee, and leaves.

Manga Girl opens the bag and pulls out a black-and-gray hood with fuzzy ears.

"Cool," Todd says. "Now you can be Raccoon Girl. Try it on."

"Not now," she says. She shoves the hood back into the bag.

I nudge Autumn, and we shuffle into the far corner, then huddle in front of a shelf of plastic dragons. "I've been thinking . . . what if I went back to Hailey's apartment, alone, and told her I didn't need the elbow macaroni after all?"

"Why would you do that?" Autumn asks. We're whispering.

"Because it would be an excuse to talk to her again. If I could talk to her, without Todd begging for food and Manga Girl looking all weird, I think she'd see that I'm nice and—"

"Stop it, Todd!" Manga Girl cries. Todd's chasing her up the narrow aisle, carrying the bag with the new raccoon hat.

"Try it on," he pleads. "Come on, don't be shy. You cheered me when I was trying to make a basket. Now

I'm cheering you. Raccoon Girl! Raccoon Girl!" Then, with a swift motion, he reaches out, grabs the top of Manga Girl's fox hood, and yanks it right off her head.

And for the first time, I see what Manga Girl actually looks like.

A Supreme Ordeal

"No! Don't!" Manga Girl jumps away, as if Todd has dumped ice water on her head.

I've never, ever seen Manga Girl without a hat. Even in PE, when everyone else has to take off their hats, she has special permission to wear hers. I know she has medium-long, curly black hair because it always sticks out around the edges. But what has she been hiding? A big birthmark? A hideous scar from a dog bite? Can a person really have horns?

So when Todd yanks the fox hood off her head, I hold my breath with anticipation.

Then I sigh with disappointment. As far as I can tell, there's nothing wrong. She looks totally normal. Her hair is black and curly, just like I knew, she has two ears, which are shaped the way ears are supposed to be shaped, and there's nothing growing out the top of her head.

She catches me staring. Her hands fly to cover her head. Her eyes well with tears. She darts into the next aisle, out of view. And then we hear sounds of muffled crying.

We stand there for a while, unsure what to do. Todd's holding the raccoon and fox hats. A cord dangles from each. So that's how she moves the ears. Mystery solved!

"Why's she crying?" he asks us. He looks as confused as Tutu does when I wake her up in the middle of a nap.

"Todd, you know she always wears a hood," I tell him. We keep our voices low. "She's never without one. And you just ripped that right off her head. There must be a reason why she wears them."

"What's the reason?" he asks. We both look at Autumn.

Autumn shrugs. "I don't know. When did I become this group's psychologist?"

Todd's shoulders slump. "I was just playing a game."

I point to the fox hat. "She'd probably like to have that back."

"Yeah, okay." He walks around the end of the aisle. Autumn and I follow. So does William. Manga Girl's sitting on the floor in a corner with her arms wrapped around her knees. An Iron Man cutout looms next to her. She looks so different without a hat. Even though her hair's smooshed down on top from wearing the fox hat, she's still pretty. But seriously, she's the second person to cry at my sleepover. That means that almost half the people at my sleepover have cried. I sure hope the Haileys don't hear that statistic.

Todd lays the fox hat at her feet. "Hey, I'm sorry. I didn't mean to make you cry."

Manga Girl stops hugging her knees. "Yeah, okay," she grumbles. She's not crying anymore. She grabs the fox hat and sticks it back on her head. Then she arranges her cape so it hangs over her shoulders.

"Why'd you freak out?" Todd asks.

She crisscrosses her legs. "Because now you know the truth."

"What truth?"

"That I don't have horns."

I gasp. "You know people say that about you?"

"Of course." She points to the fabric ears. "I listen, remember."

Right. The eavesdropping thing. But something doesn't make sense. "You don't want people to see your head because you *want* people to think you have horns?"

"Sure. Or pointed ears, or a gaping hole. Whatever. It gives me an interesting story. It gives me a supreme ordeal. Otherwise, I'm boring." She readjusts the hat. "I started wearing hoods in kindergarten because I liked it. We all wore costumes back then, remember?"

"Yeah, I remember," Todd says. "There was this pair of Batman pajamas that I wore everywhere."

"Me too," Autumn says, "only it wasn't Batman pajamas. It was a Snow White princess dress."

"I had a green fairy skirt that I loved so much I even wore it to bed," I recall.

"Well, that's when Uncle Galaxy got me reading Critter League," Manga Girl explains. "Whenever those girls put on their hats, they get superpowers. I wanted to be like them, so I started wearing their hats."

"How come the teachers don't make you take them off?" I ask.

"Because I'm the one who started the rumor about the horns." She smiles proudly. "The teachers seem too embarrassed to ask me about it, so no one ever tells me to take the hats off."

I try to wrap my head around Manga Girl's confession. All this time we thought she had some kind of freakish deformity. And she wanted us to think that. She wanted people to believe she was different in a weird way. That made her stand out, made her less boring. She wanted to create her own story and make it fantastical.

I think I can relate. I want to create my own story, too, but it's not working out the way I planned. "You have pretty hair," I tell her. "You should let people see it. I'd kill to have hair like yours." Which is totally true. Mine is so straight nothing makes it wavy—not an iron, not curlers. Tutu says my hair is as slick as a monk seal's back.

"Thanks?" Manga Girl looks surprised that I complimented her.

"And I don't think you're boring," Todd tells her. "You're a published artist. That's cool!" William nods.

"Is that why you always sit in the corner?" Autumn asks.

Manga Girl gets to her feet. "If I'm in the corner, no one can sneak up on me and pull off my hat." She straightens her cape. "But now the secret's out of the bag. I suppose you'll all go back to school and tell everyone."

"No, we won't," Todd says.

Will I spread Manga Girl's secret, or will I keep it? I want to think about that for a moment, but Manga Girl doesn't give me the chance. She walks to the counter and grabs a pack of Hi-Chew candy, cherry flavored. "This is my ingredient."

Have none of these people ever eaten soup? Popcorn *and* candy?

"Hey, Uncle Galaxy," Manga Girl calls. "We're going now."

"Already?" he asks as he steps out of his office. "Did you find what you were looking for?"

"Yeah." She holds up the candy.

Uncle Galaxy chuckles. "Your favorite. I should have guessed. Okay, good luck with the rest of your scavenger quest," he says as he opens the front door for us. But once we're on the sidewalk, he calls, "Wait." He hands the Captain America shield to William. "You keep this. Silence may be golden, but every once in a while, it needs to be shattered."

William looks at him and nods.

Manga Girl sticks the pack of Hi-Chew into Todd's backpack.

"Who's next?" Todd asks.

For the first time since leaving our apartment building, William takes the lead. He starts walking down the street, real fast, like he has something important to do. Manga Girl follows.

Todd shrugs. "Guess he's next."

I admit, I'm dying to see William's special place. So

far, the scavenger hunt has been eye-opening, that's for sure.

It's dinnertime, and that miniature Snickers isn't going to hold me much longer. Can you eat uncooked pasta right from the box? Even the used popcorn is starting to sound good.

It's definitely dark now, but lots of people are out, and most of the shops are still open, so it doesn't feel dangerous. But it's getting cold, and my thin raincoat won't be enough if it gets much colder. Todd's only wearing basketball shorts and a T-shirt, but he doesn't complain. Manga Girl's wrapped up in her cape. She looks warm. And Autumn's parka is zipped to her chin, the hood nestled around her face.

"Hey, William," I call after five blocks of walking. "We agreed not to leave the neighborhood, remember?" He doesn't turn around. Shield in hand, he walks even faster. His outfit makes no sense—a fur hat, a plaid coat, and now a plastic shield. I really hope Mom won't force me to spend more time with him. She likes inviting neighbors over for pineapple upside-down cake. She'll probably do that with William and his mom, just to be nice. But one-sided conversations are simply no fun.

"That was a really good idea about the shield, don't you think?" Todd asks Autumn.

"It could potentially work."

"This whole night has been great," he says. "I got to practice shooting baskets in front of a crowd. William has something to help him talk. And Manga Girl found out that we like her even though she's normal."

I'm not ready to be added to the "We like Manga Girl" list. It doesn't matter to me if she wears a hat or a frying pan on her head. She still drew that mean cartoon, and she still hasn't apologized. But I do understand how she feels—how she wants to be noticed.

Deep in thought, I slow my pace and fall behind. Todd and Autumn walk ahead of me. They look funny together. She's half his height. Hey, why are Autumn and Todd walking together? Is he laughing? This could be serious. If Todd and Autumn start dating, then I'll have to see Todd all the time. They'll eat lunch together. They'll hang out after school. She'll want to go to his games. I'll be a third wheel, and then I'll lose . . .

I'll lose the only friend I have.

I push between them. "Hey, Todd, are you and Hailey Chun friends?"

"Sure, I guess. We talk sometimes at school."

"Really? Will you tell her that I'm nice?"

He shrugs. "I don't know, Leilani. Are you nice?"

I gasp. "What kind of question is that? Of course I'm nice."

"Seems to me that putting people on a 'DO NOT invite' list isn't nice."

"Are you still mad about that?" I wave my hand through the air, as if brushing the whole thing away. "It was just a silly mix-up." I'm about to say *Right, Autumn?*, but when I look over at her, she looks away. She doesn't like lying about stuff.

We pass a Thai restaurant. My stomach growls. "So, Todd, are you having fun at my sleepover?"

"Sure."

I dart in front of him and start walking backward. "Then will you tell Hailey Chun that I have amazing sleepovers and she should come to the next one?"

"She told you she didn't want to," he says.

"But maybe you can convince her, since you two are friends."

He and Autumn stop walking. He folds his arms. "Look, Leilani. I'll make you a deal. I'll tell Hailey that you're nice and she should come to your sleepover if you admit I'm your cousin."

"Okay. You're my cousin."

"No, you have to do it at school, in front of *everyone*."

"What? Why?"

"Forget it." He starts walking again. Autumn blinks at me.

"Okay, fine," I say as I whip around. "I'll—"

Todd, Manga Girl, and William are standing in front of a brick building, staring up at a sign. A bad feeling settles in my stomach, but it isn't hunger. The sign reads:

Capitol Hill Cat Hospital

Beautiful Belle

"Is your cat in there?" I ask.

William nods. He walks up the steps and tries the door, but it's locked. He starts knocking. Todd, Manga Girl, Autumn, and I watch from the sidewalk. "I've seen him carry his cat around, in a carrier," I tell them. "Her name is Belle."

"What's wrong with her?" Manga Girl asks.

"I don't know. I only saw her a few times. She's black, with yellow eyes."

William presses his hand to the door's windowpane and peers through the glass. It's dark inside.

"Hey, dude, it's closed," Todd calls out. "You want to choose a different place?"

At that moment, a huge shower hits, pouring the way it does in Seattle, like buckets over your head. It's the kind of rain that passes quickly, but it can soak right through jeans and shoes, so we hurry up the steps and squeeze into the doorway, under the eaves. The big, fat drops ricochet off the sidewalk and make so much noise I can't even hear the buses and cars as they pass by.

During the shower, William keeps his face pressed to the glass, staring into the hospital's lobby. Across the street, a few people huddle in a covered bus stop. Others run into a grocery store. About a minute later, the rain stops and I can hear again.

"I hope your cat doesn't have cancer," Todd says. He's standing so close to me my back is pressed up against the wall and his chest is in my face. "My dog got cancer and died."

"Jeez, Todd, don't say stuff like that," I tell him, pushing him away before he realizes that this is the perfect opportunity to trap me in one of his toxic fart clouds. "William's cat's not going to die from cancer." But really, what do I know? As William stands there, looking into the dark hospital, I start to feel sorry for him. It's bad enough he can't talk to people, but now his cat is sick. What if she does die? What would that do to him?

I've never had a cat or a dog. Mom says that her work schedule is too busy for a pet. But when I was eight,

I begged and begged, and finally she let me get a hamster. He was cute, with a black face and a white spot on his butt. I named him Spot, and even though he made my room smell funky, I really liked watching him waddle on his wheel. Autumn and I built mazes for him, out of books, but it didn't matter if there was a piece of lettuce at the end of the maze, or a cookie, he still only waddled at one speed—super slow.

But then, two months after I bought him, he died. Just like that. I found him in the corner of his cage. I never cried so hard in my life. Mom was working an odd day shift, so Tutu put Spot into an empty coconut macaroon box, and we went to the pet store. "We want our money back," she told the manager.

"Is something wrong?" he asked.

"The mouse died after two months," Tutu told him.

He opened the box. "I'm very sorry. But this isn't a mouse. It's a hamster, and like most rodents, they don't live very long."

Tutu stomped over to the hamster cages and pointed an angry finger. "I don't see any warning signs on these cages—'Warning, these things don't live long!' Why don't you tell people that? So girls, like my granddaughter, won't get their hearts broken!"

He gave us back the money. And a coupon for a new hamster. But we didn't get one. I didn't want to feel that sad ever again.

I stand next to William and peer through the glass. The reception room is dark, but light trickles under the doorway at the end of the hall. "Hey, someone might be back there," I say. I start knocking. Manga Girl starts knocking, too. Then Todd and Autumn join us. We're pounding so loud I worry a passerby might call the police.

The hallway door flies open, and a man in jeans and a white shirt darts out. He squints at us, then hurries up the hall. When he opens the front door, I'm sure he's going to yell at us for making so much noise. "What do you . . . ?" He pauses when he sees William. "Oh, hi, William. Are you here to visit Belle?"

William nods.

"She's sleeping right now. But . . . why don't you kids come in out of the cold?"

Our sneakers squeak on the linoleum floor. It smells gross in here, like cleaning spray and kitty litter. It's warm, though, and that's nice, but my heart starts pounding because I really don't like hospitals. I hate them. It doesn't matter if they're for people or cats. They're places where things die. Tutu was in the hospital two years ago with pneumonia. I'll never forget how she looked lying in that bed, with a tube dripping something into her veins. Mom and I both cried because we were really scared that we were going to lose her. "Don't worry," Tutu had said. "Killing me is like trying to bend a coconut tree. It's a really hard thing to do."

As we gather in the waiting room, the man turns on a light. "I don't usually let people in after hours, but"— he puts a hand on William's shoulder—"I know how much you care about Belle. Go ahead. You know where to find her. But be very quiet. She needs her rest."

William sets the shield on a bench, then walks down the hall and disappears into the back room.

"I'm Dr. Kevin," the man says, shaking each of our hands. "It was nice of you to come down here with William."

"What's wrong with his cat?" Manga Girl asks.

"Cancer," the doctor says.

Todd groans. "Crud. I knew it. That's the worst."

"Yes, it can be fatal." Dr. Kevin slides his glasses up his long nose. "Belle had surgery to remove the tumor, and now she's undergoing chemotherapy to kill any remaining cancer cells. William's been very dedicated to Belle's recovery. He catches a taxi and brings her here for treatment." My eyes widen. So that explains why William always has the cat carrier in the elevator. "He usually takes her home after the treatment, but she didn't react well to this last round."

"That sucks," Todd says.

"Is she going to die?" Manga Girl asks.

"Well, if this last treatment doesn't stop the cancer, then, yes, she'll die. She might not even make it through the night."

"Oh, poor little thing," Autumn whispers.

"But if she does wake up and start eating, then that will be a very good sign, and we'll know in a few weeks if the cancer is gone."

"Is there anything we can do?" Manga Girl asks.

The doctor smiles sadly. "That's a very nice question, but we've done everything medical science knows of. Now it's up to fate." He glances down the hallway, then back at us. "William's lucky to have so many friends. It's hard to find a good therapy cat. If Belle dies, well, I think he'll need his friends more than ever."

I swallow hard. I was feeling pretty bad about the whole cancer thing, but now I feel even worse. We aren't William's friends. We barely know him. And I planned on never hanging out with him again. "Therapy cats are hard to find?" I ask.

"Yes, because cats can be tricky." Dr. Kevin points to a poster on the wall, a photo of an old lady with a cat on her lap. The old lady is in a wheelchair, and both she and the cat are smiling. "Animals help people feel calm. Petting a dog or a cat is a natural way to lower stress, for all of us. Seniors, like the lady in the poster, are often alone, so having a pet makes them feel less lonely. And a pet can help lower anxiety. Dogs work well as therapy pets because they are naturally social. They want to interact with humans. But cats are difficult because they tend to be aloof and prefer to be solitary. Belle is different because she likes being held. She wants to be by William's side."

"That's so sweet," Autumn says.

The phone on the reception desk rings. "Go ahead and have a seat," Dr. Kevin tells us. Then he answers the phone.

Manga Girl, Todd, and Autumn all take seats in the waiting room. Manga Girl starts working on another one of her secret cartoons. Autumn picks up a magazine called *Cat Fancy*, and Todd looks over her shoulder while she thumbs through the pages. Now they're *reading* together? At this rate, they'll be engaged by the end of the night!

While Dr. Kevin talks on the phone, giving instructions on how to put eyedrops into a cat's eyes without getting clawed to pieces, I tiptoe down the hall and peer into the back room. It looks like an operating room, with a table, a sink, and a bunch of medical supplies on the shelves. Six metal cages are stacked against the back wall. William stands in front of one. I can barely see the black cat, who's lying on her side. William has stuck his fingers through the bars and is stroking the cat's ear. Her eyes are closed. There's a white cat in another cage who's making wheezing sounds. But there's another sound in the room.

Whispering.

William's lips are moving. He's *talking* to Belle. He's telling her that she'll be okay. That she'll be coming home. And that he loves her.

For once in my life, I don't want to eavesdrop. I slip away from the door before he sees me. I lean against the wall. I'm beginning to understand the boy from the third floor. Those times in the elevator when he ignored me, when he looked so sad holding the cat carrier. He wasn't being rude because he didn't like me. He has stuff going on.

It seems that we all have stuff going on.

I go back to the lobby and sit with the others. Manga Girl's still drawing. Todd has given up on *Cat Fancy* and is tossing a cat toy from hand to hand. Autumn's reading a pamphlet on fleas and ticks. Dr. Kevin hangs up the phone and begins to shuffle through files. I don't say anything about William talking to his cat. I know I've seen something important, but it feels private. Like it isn't my place to tell anyone.

"What does *Belle* mean?" I ask Autumn, wishing I had my name book.

"It's French," she says. "It means 'beautiful.'"

William comes back about ten minutes later. His eyes are red. It's official. More than half the people at my sleepover ended up crying.

"I bet you could use another one of these." Dr. Kevin hands William a little plastic plant container. The plant growing in it looks like a clump of regular old grass, the kind you'd find on a playground. "It'll help settle her stomach, just like the other times. Greens work wonders for cats." So that's why William's been in the alley with a pair of scissors. He's been collecting greens for his cat to help her feel better.

William holds up two fingers, the way little kids do when you ask them how old they are. "Two?" Dr. Kevin asks. "Okay." He gives William a second container. "I'll call your home number if anything changes—I promise. I'm here all night." Then the doctor opens the front door and ushers us out.

We stand on the stoop. William hands one of the

plants to Todd. "Is this your special ingredient? One for Belle and one for the soup?" William nods. "But it's for cats. Can we eat it?"

"It's just grass," I tell Todd. "And it couldn't taste any worse in the soup than candy or used popcorn."

"Yeah, I guess you're right." Todd sticks the plant into his backpack.

It's really dark now. "I guess we're done," I say. I'm freezing and hungry. "Let's go. I'll ask Tutu to order us a couple of pizzas." Todd texts my mom to tell her that we're heading back to the apartment and that everyone is fine. We walk two blocks to the bus stop, and the bus pulls up right away. We get on and grab the front seats. Todd and Manga Girl sit together. William slides into the next row. Then I sit down.

No one sits next to me.

The door closes, and the bus starts down the street.

"Hey," I say. "Where's Autumn?"

First Fight

We jump off at the next stop. Why didn't Autumn keep up with us? Is she waiting at the previous stop, or will she try to walk all the way back to my apartment? None of us is supposed to walk alone, so we need to find her. We run up the wet sidewalk as fast as we can.

"Be sure to look on both sides of the street," I say. "Just in case."

But we don't find her. What could have happened? I start thinking about all sorts of bad things, like being abducted by a stranger, or falling through a sewer grate, or getting struck by a sudden bout of amnesia! Any of those things *could* happen.

Autumn. Where are you?

I'm breathing pretty hard when we reach the place

where we last saw her. And there she is, sitting on the front steps of the cat hospital. "Autumn?" I'm gasping for air. "What are you doing?"

"William forgot his shield," she says. It's lying on her lap. "I told you I was going back inside to get it. But when I got outside, you'd all disappeared." She looks hurt, like we left her behind on purpose.

"I didn't hear you," I explain. Autumn's voice is so quiet, and the street noise on Capitol Hill is constant. "I thought you were right behind me."

"That was nice of you to remember the shield," Manga Girl tells her.

"Yeah, super nice," Todd says.

Autumn gets to her feet. Then she offers the shield to William. During the run, his fur hat fell off. Now it dangles from his hand. His blond hair is smooshed into weird patterns, and a big clump is flattened against his forehead. Major hat head.

"Don't you want it?" Autumn asks, still holding the shield.

I wonder if William left the shield behind on purpose. After all, it's just a plastic toy. Maybe he was too polite to refuse it when Uncle Galaxy gave it to him. Or maybe he did forget it. I have no idea what he's thinking. I can't read him any better than those vocab cards in Reading Lab.

He puts on his hat, then takes the shield. He looks at Autumn, then at the shield, then back at Autumn. He shuffles in place. With his lips pressed together, real tight, he looks like he's trying to hold back a burp. *Wait. Does he want to say something?* But there aren't any doors to hide behind. No aisles blocking our view. His hands begin to tremble.

"It's okay," Autumn whispers. "You can do it."

William lifts the shield slowly until it's in front of his face. *Whoa! Is he going to do it? Is he going to say something?* Todd's mouth falls open. Manga Girl's fox ears straighten. Autumn and I hold our breath. It's like watching a suspense movie. All we need is that music from *Jaws*. So I play it in my head—*dah dum, dah dum, dah dum.*

"Thank you."

William Worth, the boy from the third floor, speaks two words on the sidewalk that night, with only a thin piece of plastic protecting him. It's not a miracle or anything like that, but it's *something*.

He lowers the shield. His face is blotchy and sweaty, as if he just ran a marathon. "You're welcome," Autumn tells him.

Todd slaps him on the back. "Dude, that was amazing."

Manga Girl bounces on her toes. "I knew it would work!"

"That *was* amazing," I say. And I mean it. I don't know much about Captain America's shield, but I'm gonna guess he never used it to fight selective mutism.

A piece of newspaper dances down the sidewalk, pushed by the sudden cold wind. I pull up the collar on my raincoat. "We should go." I wonder if Tutu is waiting. "Come on, Autumn." I start walking toward the bus stop, but Autumn doesn't move. "What's the matter?"

She crosses her arms and frowns. "You forgot about me."

"No, I didn't. I didn't hear you say you were going back into the hospital to get the shield. That's why we got on the bus without you."

"You forgot about *my turn*."

"Huh?" What's she talking about?

"Whoa, she's right," Todd says. "Autumn hasn't had a turn yet. She hasn't taken us to her special place." Autumn tightens her arms, as if giving herself a hug. She sinks deeper into her coat.

Oh crud, it's true.

"If Leilani hadn't been in such a hurry to get home, we wouldn't have forgotten," Manga Girl tells her.

"Hey, why is this my fault? I didn't forget," I insist, even though I did. There's been so much going on, like all the crying and all the cat drama—it was an honest mistake. "I just thought that maybe, well, maybe you didn't really care about going to a special place and getting an ingredient. You know, because magic isn't real and there's no such thing as a moon goddess." Autumn's round eyes get even rounder. She always knows when I'm lying. "Yeah, okay, so I forgot," I confess. "I'm hungry. And I'm tired. And Tutu's going to get worried if we stay out any later. That's why I was in a hurry. I'm sorry. I'm really, really sorry."

"I know the real reason why you want to get back," Manga Girl says, flinging her cape behind her shoulders. "You want to know what Hailey Chun is doing at her sleepover. You wanted to spend tonight with her and not with us. You'd rather spy on the Haileys than give Autumn a turn."

Todd shakes his head. "Jeez, that's cold, cuz."

I gasp. "That is completely and totally not true." Why is everyone ganging up on me? "I wasn't thinking about Hailey Chun. I don't care what she's doing." Oddly enough, at this moment, that's absolutely true. I turn my frustration on Manga Girl. "Why don't you go and draw another cartoon, this time about how horrid I am that I forgot my best friend?"

After a long sigh, Autumn slumps onto the steps. I throw myself next to her. "Don't listen to them. Yeah, okay, so I forgot about your turn, but I didn't do it on purpose. We've been best friends since that day in the nurse's office when you . . . you know, since *that* day. I would never try to hurt your feelings. I think maybe I forgot about your turn because, well, sometimes you're . . ."

"Invisible?" She blinks at me.

"No, not invisible." I pull my raincoat over my knees to try to stay warm. "Just because Uncle Galaxy said that, it doesn't mean it's true. You're quiet. *Super* quiet. Sometimes I don't hear you."

The hood of Autumn's raincoat lies open against her back, making a nest for her curls. In the dim light, I can barely see any of her freckles. "You didn't forget about my turn because I'm quiet," she says. "You forgot because I've been a willing participant in this pattern of behavior."

I scoot closer to her. "What do you mean? What *pattern of behavior*?"

"It's true what Tanisha said, about me being in your shadow."

I gulp. Her voice is so serious. "I don't know what you're talking about."

Autumn puts her hand on my knee. "It's not your fault, Leilani. It's mine. I gave myself the power of invisibility because it's easier for me to follow than to confront. That's why I always let you make the decisions."

I get dizzy all of a sudden. There are so many emotions rushing over me it feels like a tidal wave. I'm hurt that Hailey Chun doesn't like me, sad that William's cat is sick, and worried that Tutu is going to call the police if we don't show up pretty soon. Also, I feel really stupid that I made the "DO NOT invite" list in the first place. But most of all, I'm upset that Autumn is upset. My stomach starts to ache. You can try to put emotions into separate compartments, but unlike a crustless cheese sandwich and perfectly peeled orange slices, emotions spill over and get all mixed up. "I . . . I . . ." I don't know what to say.

A gust of wind sweeps over us. Autumn shivers, then puts her hands in her pockets. "Leilani, I want to tell you how I feel about something—something you do that's been bothering me."

This is starting to get weird. Are we having a fight? We never, ever have fights. "Can we talk about this later?" I whisper, because Todd, Manga Girl, and William clearly have nothing better to do than to stand here and watch us. "When we're *alone*?"

"No. If I don't say this now, I might never say it." She takes a long, deep breath. Then she looks into my eyes. My stomachache gets worse. The way she's looking at me, I can tell she's about to deliver some really bad news. Mom looked the same way when she told me that Tutu was in the hospital. "We're supposed to be best friends, but you're obsessed with the Haileys. You know everything about them, their schedules, what they do on weekends, where they go shopping, what they wear. We spend most of our time at lunch talking about them. Well, *you* talk about them. I mostly listen. It hurts my feelings. It seems that you . . ." She pauses. "That you . . ." She swallows hard. William steps forward and offers her the shield. She puts it in front of her face. "That you would rather be friends with them than with me."

"What? That's crazy!" I feel a sudden rush of relief. I pull the shield from her hands. "Is that why you're mad at me? Because you think I'd choose the Haileys over you? No way! Never!"

"Really?" she says.

"Really!"

"Then why do you spend so much time talking about them?" Manga Girl asks.

"Well, in the first place, *Tanisha*, this is none of your business," I snap. "And in the second place, it's true. I'd like to have a bigger group of friends. What's wrong with that? Wouldn't you like to have more friends?"

"If I had a best friend as nice as Autumn, I'd be happy," Manga Girl says. "One true friend is better than a bunch of false friends."

She's right, *again*. "I am happy that Autumn's my best friend. But . . ." I'm about to admit how I feel. Forget Hawaiian luau. The theme of my sleepover is "Admit your fears in front of everyone." I don't think that's going to catch on as a trend. "But Autumn leaves Seattle every other weekend to go visit her dad, and I'm on my own. I just thought it would be nice to be friends with the Haileys so I wouldn't be alone on those weekends. I miss Autumn when she's gone."

"You do?" Autumn blinks at me.

"Yeah. But that doesn't mean I want a new best friend." I put my arm around Autumn's shoulders. Have I really been ignoring her? A parade of lunches runs through my mind. In each one, Autumn is chewing in her squirrel-like way and I'm talking.

About the Haileys.

Everyone's right. I've been totally obsessed. "It doesn't matter anyway. The Haileys hate me." Tears well in my eyes. Oh, jeez, now *I'm* crying! "I'm sorry. I never wanted to hurt your feelings. Never. Next week, you get to be in charge of the conversation at lunch. We'll talk about whatever you want. You know, science and stuff like that." I wipe my nose on my sleeve. "And we'll do that thing you wanted to do." She's been talking about something all week. Come on, Leilani, what is it? "That exhibit at the science center. About the brain."

Finally, Autumn smiles.

"Group hug!" Todd yells, and before I can stop him, he's squeezing the life out of me and Autumn.

"I don't hug," Manga Girl says. William doesn't join in, either. He's looking up at the cat hospital door with a pained expression, like he has a really bad headache. I twist away from Todd.

"Okay, everyone, listen up," I say. "It's Autumn's turn, and we're going to her special place, but we've really got to go now, because if we stay out much later, Tutu will spew lava like Kilauea."

Autumn jumps to her feet. "Don't worry, my special place is right by your apartment."

I grab her arm. "It's not Hailey Chun's, is it?"

"No!" She laughs. "You'll see."

22

Squirrels Like Nuts

Manga Girl draws while we wait for the bus, then during the ride, but she still won't let us see what she's creating. I use Todd's phone to call home but get the answering machine. "Tutu," I say, "we'll be back soon. Don't worry."

The bus drops us off one block from my apartment, right in front of the Capitol Hill International Market, which is a mini market with all sorts of specialty foods. I've been here a million times with Tutu. It's her favorite place to shop because the owners, Mr. and Mrs. Wong, include Hawaiian foods in their store. Tutu buys things like guava jam, hibiscus honey lemon tea, Kona coffee, macadamia shortbread cookies, papaya seed dressing, and coconut syrup, which she loves to pour over vanilla ice cream.

"This is my special place," Autumn explains.

"How come?" Todd asks.

"I don't get to see my grandparents very often, so Tutu is like a step-grandma to me. Whenever I go to Leilani's house, Tutu brings us here for treats. The first time she did, she introduced me to chocolate-covered macadamia nuts, and now they're my favorite candy."

I remember that day. We were in kindergarten, brand-new friends, and while Autumn's mom and my mom chatted in the kitchen, Tutu walked Autumn and me to the market. Mr. Wong had bought a new shave-ice machine, and he was handing out samples. Tutu informed him that shave ice was a Hawaiian invention. He said the Chinese invented it, because they invented everything. He and Tutu got into a big argument, but eventually we ordered, and I got passion fruit and Autumn got strawberry, because she was scared about trying a new flavor. That was when Tutu said, "Come look at this, Autumn. These nuts are the most special nuts in all of Hawaii." And then she told Autumn the same story she'd told me when I tried my first macadamia nut. "You have to wait ten long years for the tree to mature. Then the nuts grow, but you can't pick them from the tree. You have to wait for the tree to offer you the nuts, by dropping them to the ground. Then each nut is carefully gathered and given the respect it deserves. Even a nut has mana." She bought Autumn an entire box, and she's been buying them for Autumn ever since.

We are about to go into the store when the glass door opens and the Haileys walk out. They are each holding a shave ice and wearing their plastic leis.

"Hey, Todd," Hailey Chun says, ignoring the rest of us.

"Hey, Hailey," he says back. "You guys are eating snow cones in the middle of winter? That's cool."

"Since my theme is Hawaiian luau, I thought we'd come down here and get some shave ice." She smiles at him. Her ice is bright blue. "What are you doing?"

"We're still on that scavenger hunt," he tells her.

"Oh, that's right. Leilani's sleepover. Are you having *fun*?" She says the word *fun* in a snippy way. Then she looks at the other five Haileys and rolls her eyes. I cringe.

Manga Girl steps in front of me. "For your information, Hailey, we are having *fun*. Lots of *fun*. It's the best scavenger hunt ever. Too bad you weren't on the 'DO NOT invite' list, because, apparently, that's the list to be on."

"What are you talking about?" Hailey asks with a sneer.

"We're making magic soup," Todd tells her. "We have one more ingredient to collect."

Heyley MacDonald steps forward. "Magic soup?" Her lips are orange, and she's shivering. "What's that?"

Autumn pushes some curls from her face. "It's blessed by the moon goddess." She sounds absolutely certain of this fact.

"That sounds amazing," Hayley Ranson says.

"It sounds stupid." Hailey Chun begins to cross the street. The others follow, except for Hayley Ranson, who's looking at me.

She grips her lime-green shave ice. "Do you think—?"

"Hayley!" Hailey Chun yells.

Hayley Ranson hurries to join her.

When they are out of earshot, I turn to Manga Girl. I can't believe she stood up for me. Why would she do that? I also can't believe that I'm about to thank the girl who uses me for "social commentary" in her cartoons, but sometimes you just have to swallow your pride. "Thanks for telling Hailey that you're having fun at my sleepover. But you don't have to lie for me."

"I didn't lie," she says. Then, with a *whoosh*, she flies into the store.

"Hello, Leilani. Hello, Autumn," Mrs. Wong calls.

She's at the counter, next to the cash register. "Where's Tutu?"

"She's waiting for us at home," I tell her.

"We close in ten minutes!" Mr. Wong bellows. He's mopping the floor. "Ten minutes, so finish shopping. Don't take too long."

"He's cranky because we just had six girls in here buying shave ice," Mrs. Wong explains. "The machine sprayed ice everywhere. I don't know why they want to eat ice on such a cold night. And I don't know why they all have the same name."

"No more ice!" Mr. Wong hollers. "We close in five minutes."

"Autumn needs something," I explain, stepping back so Autumn can talk.

Autumn stands on tiptoe and folds her hands on the counter. "Mrs. Wong, do you have any chocolate-covered macadamia nuts? I don't need a whole box. I just need one. Do they come individually wrapped?"

"Just one?" Mrs. Wong looks over her glasses. "But what about your friends?"

"It's for a project," Autumn says. "Just one will do. We're making magic soup."

Mrs. Wong nods thoughtfully. "Magic soup." She

smiles. "I have an open box in my office. Since you are a loyal customer, I'll share one with you." She hurries away, and just as Mr. Wong hollers "We're closed!" she's back. She hands Autumn a little sandwich bag with a single chocolate-covered macadamia nut inside.

"Thank you," Autumn says. Then she looks at me. "We can go now."

Even though I'm hungry, and tired, and worried that Tutu will be worried, I don't leave. Standing in that market, surrounded by the foods from Tutu's homeland, I realize something. Each of my sleepover guests has collected an ingredient for the soup that is meaningful to them. But that box of elbow macaroni isn't important to me. Not anymore.

"Mrs. Wong, do you have taro root?" I ask.

"Certainly."

"We're closed!" Mr. Wong yells from the back room.

"Could I get just a tiny piece? That's all I need."

"Let me guess," she says, putting a finger to her chin. "For the magic soup?" I nod. She reaches into a drawer and takes out a small knife. Then we walk over to the produce aisle. I find the taro right away. It's shaped like a potato, only the skin is a deep, dark brown. Mrs. Wong cuts it in half. "Here you are. No charge. Now go, before my husband's head pops off."

"Thank you, Mrs. Wong!" we all say, except for William, of course.

We hurry to my apartment building. But while the others wait in the lobby, I run over to Hailey Chun's building and hand the box of elbow macaroni to the doorman. "Could you give this back to Hailey? I don't need it anymore."

Tutu's in the kitchen. She's wearing her pink bathrobe and making herself a cup of tea. "You're back," she says, not seeming one bit worried. "How was your adventure?"

"It was great!" Todd exclaims. "We got all the stuff for the soup."

We pile the coats and shield onto a chair. Then Todd unpacks the ingredients and sets them on the kitchen table. Tutu pulls her cat-eye glasses from her bathrobe pocket and slides them onto her nose. "Candy, grass, popcorn, a chocolate-covered macadamia nut?" She picks up the root. "Who chose taro?"

"Me," I tell her. The skin around her eyes crinkles. She's smiling! It's not very often that Tutu smiles that big, with her whole face.

"Hey, do I smell pizza?" Todd charges into the living room.

"I thought you'd be hungry," Tutu explains.

Hungry? I'm famished! Two pizza boxes sit on the coffee table, along with paper plates, napkins, and sodas.

"Cheese!" Todd belts. "My favorite!" He grabs a slice, then sticks another slice on top.

"I'm not sleeping next to him tonight," I whisper to Autumn.

Manga Girl opens the second box. "This one's Hawaiian."

Autumn carefully chooses a slice and sets it neatly on a plate. "I'll never understand why it's called Hawaiian if it's made with Canadian bacon."

Tutu lets us know that she's going to bed and that we aren't to disturb her unless King Kamehameha himself rises from the dead and asks for her. "And I'm not cleaning up your messes." Then her bedroom door closes.

We stuff our faces. I eat two slices of Hawaiian, then split a third slice with Autumn. She nibbles on the cheesy part, avoiding the crust. When my stomach feels like it might burst, I lean against the couch pillows. Manga Girl's still eating. So is Todd. William's taken off his hat, but he sits cross-legged on the floor, staring at his plate. That's when I realize he hasn't eaten a bite. I'm not sure what to do to help him feel better.

Manga Girl looks up from her pizza and watches William for a moment. Her fox ears twitch. Then she grabs her sketchbook. "Hey, William, I know how to cheer you up. Wanna see the cartoon I drew of Belle?" She opens the book and holds it up. We all gasp. She's going to let us see? We push our plates aside and scoot closer.

In the first frame, a black cat is sitting alone, looking very angry. A chain hangs from the cat's neck, and at the end of the chain is a big metal ball, and on that ball is the word *Cancer*. In the next few frames, a boy with a fur hat and big plaid coat walks up to the cat. He's holding a pair of wire cutters, and on the cutters is the word *Love*. The boy cuts the chain. In the last frame, the boy is holding the cat, who is now free of the cancer. Both the boy and the cat are smiling.

"Wow, that's really good," Todd says. "It looks just like William."

Manga Girl signs the bottom corner, then tears the cartoon from her sketchbook and hands it to William. He manages a half smile, but his pale eyes are still full of sadness. I'm not mad at Manga Girl anymore. I don't really care what she drew of me, because the cartoon of Belle and William is the nicest cartoon I've ever seen.

"Did you draw one of me?" Todd asks.

"Yep." She flips through the pages, then shows us the drawing. There's Todd, with his long skinny legs, short dark hair, and uniform. He stands next to an empty bench, holding a basketball. Icicles hang from the bench. I furrow my brow, trying to figure it out.

"Oh, I get it," Todd says after a minute. "It's got icicles because I'm not warming it anymore." He laughs. She signs it and gives it to him.

"I made one of you." Now it's Autumn's turn. Manga Girl turns the page and shows us a drawing of a girl with lots of curls and super big eyes. She's wearing a hat, like the ones Manga Girl wears, but it has squirrel ears. She also has a big, bushy squirrel tail. She stands next to a nest that's filled with macadamia nuts. Autumn squeals because it makes her so happy. Manga Girl signs it and hands it over.

Each drawing is better than the last. She's really good.

"What about Leilani?" Todd asks. "Did you draw one of her?"

My mood suddenly sours. I narrow my eyes at Manga Girl. *Don't you dare show them that mean cartoon*, I think. But apparently, reading minds isn't one of Fox Girl's superpowers, because she opens the sketchbook to that horrid drawing of the letters attacking me. While everyone else leans forward, I fall back against the pillows. "Don't bother signing it," I grumble. "I don't want it."

Todd takes another bite of pizza. "How come?"

"She's making fun of the fact that I have trouble reading."

Autumn nudges me. "You should look at it. It's very nice."

Nice? I take the drawing from Manga Girl. *The worst part is the waiting, so I might as well get this over with,* I tell myself.

The girl in the cartoon has long black hair and is kind of plump, like me, but she wears a cape. In the first frame, the letters are attacking her. But in the other frames, she's wrestling them to the ground and tying them up, the way a cowboy ties a calf at a rodeo. In the last frame, she stands proudly on top of a mountain of letters, her hands on her hips. A conquering hero.

"Thanks," I say with surprise.

We cram onto the couch together, even William, and we look through Manga Girl's sketchbook. She's drawn a cartoon of the Haileys as identical robots. There's a drawing of Mr. Pine putting all his students to sleep because he's so boring. There are some realistic drawings of foxes, raccoons, and cats. There are a bunch of self-portraits of Manga Girl in her different hats. She turns to the last page, where she's started a new self-portrait. This final drawing is different from the others because the lines are darker and there's no hat on her head. As we stare at the drawing, a beam of light shines on our faces.

"Look!" For the first time all night, Autumn's voice is so loud it startles everyone. She points out the window. The clouds have drifted away and a crescent moon hangs above Hailey Chun's apartment, like a smile—its light shining right through my window. A shiver of excitement dances up my spine.

"Do you guys still want to make the soup?" I ask.

Moonlight Wishes

I turn the burner to medium and warm up the broth. Then I take the lid off the pot. Todd dumps in all the popcorn, including some unpopped kernels. Using my mom's cooking shears, William snips some blades of wheatgrass, then sprinkles them onto the surface, where they float. The macadamia nut sinks to the bottom, along with the Hi-Chew. I dice the taro root with a steak knife, drop in the pieces, then stir with a wooden spoon. As the Hi-Chew dissolves, the golden broth turns pink. "Blech! This soup is gonna taste disgusting."

"I don't think taste is what matters," Autumn says. "I think this is all about the process."

"What do you mean?" Manga Girl asks.

"The process of gathering the ingredients. Working together."

"Working as a team," Todd adds.

Autumn grabs the recipe card. I find a ladle and some paper cups. Then, after turning off the stove, I give two oven mitts to Todd so he can carry the pot. We take the stairs to the roof. The rooftop garden is one of my favorite places. There are a couple of wooden benches and a table for picnics. In the summer, some of the tenants plant tomatoes, herbs, and flowers. There's a big striped umbrella for shade and a pair of bird feeders. But it's winter, so the containers are empty and the umbrella is in storage. Luckily, the table and benches are still out.

The moon floats overhead, as if waiting for us. Todd puts the pot on the table. I remove the lid.

"What are we supposed to do now?" Todd asks.

Autumn reads the recipe card. "It says, 'Once the ingredients are added, set the soup beneath the moonlight. Ask Hina-i-ka-malama to bless the soup. Everyone makes a wish and takes a sip of soup. If all instructions are followed, the wishes will come true. Important note: The magic won't work unless everyone participates.'"

"I think Leilani should talk to Hina," Manga Girl suggests. "Since it's her family recipe."

I suddenly feel silly, standing on the roof, about to talk to a moon goddess. What am I supposed to say?

Unlike Autumn and Todd, I've never had stage fright, but with everyone looking at me, expecting some kind of amazing speech, I feel uncomfortable. And cold. Why didn't I grab my coat?

"I . . . I . . ."

"I'll do it," Todd volunteers. He steps onto one of the benches and raises his hands to the sky. Then he looks down at me. "You okay if I do it?" he asks.

"Sure," I say.

Todd turns his face to the moon. "Hey, moon goddess, lady, we made this soup and we need you to shine your beams and do whatever it is you do so our wishes will come true. We hope you'll help us out. Thanks from all of us—me, Tanisha, Autumn, William, and Leilani." He steps off. "That should do it." It wasn't poetry, but I don't think I could have done any better.

Using the ladle, I pour soup into each cup.

"Everyone, close your eyes and make a wish," Autumn whispers.

I don't close my eyes. Instead, I focus on the rooftop across the street. Last summer, Hailey Chun had a birthday party on her roof. Her family decorated the roof with strings of paper lanterns, and I could hear the music from my bedroom. For most of the school year, I've longed to become one of the Haileys. To be a member of their club. To sit with them at lunch. To go to all their parties. That could be my wish.

But my gaze drifts back to my sleepover guests, the ones from the "DO NOT invite" list. Their eyes are closed. Each looks happy, thinking about the thing they long for. But William looks like he's in pain. His eyes are squeezed super tight, his lips moving silently as he makes his wish. I know what he wants.

I close my eyes and wish and wish and wish.

"Everyone done?" I ask.

We open our eyes and pick up the cups of soup. The pink mixture looks fluorescent in the moonlight. Autumn plugs her nose. William grimaces.

"Ready, set, go!" Todd says. And we each take a sip.

"Bleh!"

"Ack!"

"Gross!"

It's really salty, probably from the popcorn, and there's a sickly sweet flavor as well. I'm not sure if I swallowed a piece of candy or a chunk of taro, but I make sure not to spit it out. I want that wish. I want it more than I've ever wanted anything.

It's done. We gathered the ingredients. We made our wishes. We drank the soup. Now it's up to the moon goddess. She'll either bless us or not.

Todd lowers his cup. "Uh-oh," he says. He puts his hand over his gut. There's a deep, rumbling sound, like a storm gathering in the distance. "The cheese pizza has landed."

With a shriek, we run toward the stairwell, leaving Todd behind to stink up the roof.

24

A New League

That Monday, after my sleepover, Autumn and I are sitting in our usual spot, next to the big round table. Autumn has her perfectly packed lunch—crustless cheese sandwich, orange slices, and apple juice. I have the cafeteria special—chicken burger and Tater Tots. The Haileys are talking, but I'm not eavesdropping. I can't stop yawning. "Jeez, I'm still tired."

"Me too," Autumn says, rubbing her eyes.

No one got any sleep at my sleepover. We spread our sleeping bags on the floor and stayed up all night, drawing cartoons, reading issues of *Critter League* that Manga Girl had brought, and talking about stuff, like the scariest movies we'd seen (I got scared just hearing the descriptions), the most embarrassing things that had ever happened to us (Autumn confessed the pee incident), and my personal favorite, how we all agreed that making new friends isn't easy. Even though William had the shield by his side the whole night, he didn't say anything. But he seemed content to listen.

When Mom came home at 4:00 AM, we were still awake, so she made us scrambled eggs before she went to bed. At some point during the night, Manga Girl took off her fox hat. I guess she was comfortable enough to let us see the real Tanisha. I was worried that we might get sick from the soup. But none of us had more than a sip. Not even Todd, who eats *everything*. It was truly the worst soup I've ever tasted, but making it was one of the craziest adventures I've ever had. It stung that Hailey Chun didn't like me, but that seemed to matter less and less as the night passed. And when I said good-bye to everyone yesterday, I realized that I hadn't looked over at Hailey's apartment. Not once!

"Hey."

I stop eating my chicken burger. Manga Girl is standing next to me, holding a sack lunch and her sketchbook. She's wearing her new raccoon hat. "Hi, Tanisha," I say.

"You can call me Manga Girl. I kind of like it." She glances at the empty chair. Does she want to eat lunch with us? I look at Autumn. Autumn shrugs.

"Uh, you wanna . . . sit with us?" I ask.

Her raccoon ears twitch. "Okay." She smiles and sits. I wonder if she's still worried that we might spill her secret. But she doesn't have to worry. I'm not going to tell anyone that the only thing Tanisha Washington is hiding beneath her hat is a totally normal head. It's her secret to do with as she wishes. Besides, it's kind of cool to have a friend who can draw *and* who people think has horns.

That's right. I used the word *friend*.

Manga Girl opens her sack lunch and pulls out a tuna sandwich, a bag of Cheetos, and some kind of soda that comes from Japan. "So, what did you guys wish for, before you ate the soup?"

"We're not supposed to tell, are we?" I ask. "I mean, the wish won't work if we tell, will it?"

"There was nothing in the instructions about secrecy," Autumn points out.

"Hey, cuz. Hey, guys." Todd pulls a chair from another table and sits next to Autumn. Her cheeks turn red, and she starts chewing on her straw. "Whatcha talking about?"

"What we wished for," Manga Girl tells him. "Before we ate the soup."

Todd grabs a couple of Cheetos. "I wished for William's cat to get better."

Manga Girl sits up straight. "So did I."

"Me too," Autumn says, her eyes widening. "I wonder how Belle is doing."

I shrug. "I don't know." I haven't seen William since saying good-bye yesterday morning. I spent the rest of the day cleaning up and hanging out on the couch with Tutu. "I'll go to his apartment after school and ask."

"That sounds good," Todd says.

"I sure hope she's better," Manga Girl says. Everyone nods.

Todd licks orange dust from his fingers. "Guess *your* wish didn't work." He stares at me.

"What do you mean?"

He tilts his head toward the big round table. "The Haileys are over there, and you're over here."

It's true. The Haileys are sitting together, laughing and talking about whatever. They're wearing their matching Converse sneakers and are dressed in a black-and-white theme. Once again, none of them bothered to send me the dress code memo. "For your information, Todd, I didn't wish anything about the Haileys."

"Really?"

"What *did* you wish?" Manga Girl asks. She sits back in her chair, her pencil poised in midair as if waiting for the next cartoon. Todd also waits. Autumn blinks at me.

What was my wish?

The night on the roof comes back to me like a movie. I stand beneath the moon, the sounds of traffic rising from the street. A crisp breeze chills my face. Then I begin my plea. *Dear Hina, goddess who looks down from the moon and blesses us with her light. I know you've never heard from me, but I promise to pay more attention to Tutu's stories, and to learn more about the land she loves. In the meantime, I'm wondering if you could do me a huge favor. Could you please wrap your arms around Belle tonight? She's very sick, and I'm sure she's scared in that hospital cage. Please make her healthy again so she can live with William and keep being his therapy cat, because he needs her. Thank you, and* Aloha pō.

"We all wished for the same thing," I tell them. Even Autumn looks shocked.

"Not about Hailey?" she asks.

"Not about Hailey," I say. It feels good to say that.

At some point, between starting the sleepover and standing on that moonlit roof, we'd become a team—united for the one person who didn't say more than a handful of words the entire night, but who needed a wish more than anyone else.

"Hi, everyone."

I gasp. Hayley Ranson has left the big round table and is now standing next to Autumn. She has a half-eaten apple in her hand. "I still wish I could have gone on that scavenger hunt with you. Are you going to do another one? Could you invite me?"

Autumn stops chewing, Manga Girl's ears perk, and Todd, well, he uses the opportunity to sneak some more Cheetos. I carefully swallow my bite of chicken burger, because if there is one moment when I don't want to choke and spray food across the table, this is certainly it. From the corner of my eye, I see movement at the big round table. Hailey Chun has turned and is watching us. I wipe the corners of my mouth with a napkin, then smile sweetly at Hayley. "Sure," I say, acting as if this is no big deal, but making sure my voice is loud enough for any eavesdroppers to hear. "I'd be happy to add your name to my invite list."

"Thanks," she says.

Hailey Chun groans in annoyance, then turns her back to us.

Hayley Ranson takes a bite of her apple. Autumn

scoots over and Hayley sits on the edge of Autumn's chair.

"What about us?" Todd asks.

"Yeah," Manga Girl says, folding her arms tightly. "Are you inviting us to your next sleepover, or are we still on the 'DO NOT invite' list?"

I laugh. "From now on, there's only one list. I promise." Then I introduce Hayley to the group. "Do you know Tanisha and Autumn? I know you already know Todd. He's my cousin."

"Hi," she says. And we spend the rest of lunch listening to Autumn tell us all about the human brain exhibit at the Pacific Science Center.

We make plans to meet there on Saturday and see it together.

The Magic of Friendship

At four o'clock that afternoon, Mom walks into the kitchen. It's her day off, so she's wearing sweatpants. "Whatcha doing?" she asks.

I'm at the sink. "I'm giving the fake plant a bath."

"Oh. That's . . . *nice*."

Using a sponge and dish soap, I scrub off all the dust and cobwebs. I grabbed the plant when I got home from school. I waited in the lobby, hoping William might ride the elevator with me. But he never showed.

"What's this?" Mom picks up the recipe card.

"Oh, Tutu gave me that." Using a dish towel, I start drying the long plastic leaves. They turn glossy and bright green. "She said she used to make it when she was a kid."

Mom reads the card. "Sleepover soup?"

"Did you ever make it?"

"No."

"That's weird, because Tutu said it was a tradition, handed down from mother to daughter. You sure you never made it?"

"I'm sure I'd remember something like this. The moon goddess?" She laughs, then sets the card aside. "Sounds like one of Tutu's stories."

"Yeah." I already figured that out. Especially because, while the other recipe cards have stains and smudges from being used so many times, this card looks brand-new, as if Tutu wrote it only a few days ago. I'm also beginning to suspect that Tutu mailed the invitations to the "DO NOT invite" list on purpose. "Mom, do you believe in magic?"

"Well, not exactly. I mean, there are things that happen that we can't explain, but I'm not sure that's magic. But there are other things that can make your life *magical*. Like love. When you love someone, your life changes in all sorts of ways, and that can feel like magic." She kisses my forehead, then grabs her coat. "I'm going to the store. How about ravioli for dinner?"

"Can we eat something Hawaiian tonight?" I ask. "I'd like to eat more Hawaiian stuff. You know, like *real* Hawaiian food. Like taro root."

Mom shudders. "Oh, I don't like taro root."

"You don't?"

She leans close to me and whispers, "Leilani, just because something grows on a beautiful island and is filled with mana, that doesn't mean it's tasty. No matter what Tutu tells you." She smiles. "How about I get some coconut ice cream for dessert?"

"Yeah, that's sounds good."

"*Aloha au iā 'oe*," she says after kissing me again.

"*Aloha au iā 'oe*."

I finish drying the plant. Tutu's on the couch, watching *Name That Tune*. "Tutu?" I call.

"Don't bother me. I'm busy."

I walk into the living room. "I just wanted to tell you that I'm going downstairs and I'll be right back." Then I pause, because there's something else I want to say. "I know what you did, with those invitations."

She peers over her cat-eye glasses at me.

"Thank you," I say.

She grunts, then turns up the TV volume. But even though she's frowning, I can tell that she's working hard to hold back a smile.

I stop at the third floor and knock on William's apartment. No one answers, so I head downstairs. When I get to the lobby, I set the plant on its stand. The green is too fluorescent to look real, but at least the plant looks new. The rest of the lobby still needs help, but this is a start. I open our mailbox. As I toss out the junk mail, a taxi pulls up to the curb and William gets out. He has the cat carrier. I rush outside. My heart starts pounding.

William sets the carrier on the sidewalk, then pays the driver. As the cab drives away, I kneel next to the carrier. Is it empty? My legs feel like Jell-O. I peer through the metal bars. Two yellow eyes stare back at me. "Hi, Belle," I say. She didn't die! She survived the chemotherapy. The doctor said that if she survived the night, she had a good chance! And that was two nights ago!

When I look up at William, he's holding the plastic shield in front of his face.

"Belle is better."

I dart to my feet. I'm so happy I hug the boy from the third floor. And he hugs me back.

Maybe Hina did hear us—I'll never know. But what I do know is that, in her funny Tutu way, my great-grandmother helped turn the worst sleepover in the history of the world into the best sleepover in the history of the world.

And that the true magic of the sleepover soup is friendship.

Author's Note

Mythology is a huge part of almost all my books. Celtic myths inspired *To Catch a Mermaid*, and the Greek and Roman stories of Hermes and of Cupid inspired *Coffeehouse Angel* and *Mad Love*. The Greek myth of King Midas influenced my YA novel *The Sweetest Spell*. When I wrote about mythological creatures in my Imaginary Veterinary series, I borrowed those creatures from all sorts of traditions, including Chinese and Japanese. So it was no surprise to me that when a new story started floating around in my head, it was based on a myth—Stone Soup. And that's when an interesting thing happened.

I researched Stone Soup and discovered that it's one of those stories that has traveled the globe and can be found, in one shape or another, in most cultures. My daughter was waiting tables at the time, and one day she was talking to a young woman named Amy who had grown up in Hawaii. Amy told her a story that her Hawaiian grandmother had often told and, lo and behold, it was about Stone Soup.

Hawaii? I didn't know much about Hawaiian myths, and I was intrigued, especially because I've spent a lot of time on those beautiful islands. I wanted to learn more, so I decided to weave Hawaiian mythology and culture into my story.

If you'd like to learn more about the legends of the Hawaiian people, the most complete resource I found is a book called *Hawaiian Mythology*, by author Martha Warren Beckwith.

Hauʻoli reading!

Acknowledgments

As is always true, there are many people who helped turn my idea into a story and then into a book. I offer my humble thanks to them.

I'm very grateful to my sister-in-law's sister, Jackie Benner Christel, for sharing all sorts of wonderful stories with me about her mother's childhood on Kauai, living on a sugarcane plantation. Those stories brought Tutu to life.

I'm grateful to still have two amazing people on my team who started with me way back when I was writing my Smells Like Dog series. Thanks to Julie Scheina for reading my early drafts before and after having a baby! And to Christine Ma for continuing to be my most beloved copyeditor.

This book brought me to a new publisher, which is always an exciting adventure. At Imprint, thanks to Nicole Otto, Natalie Sousa, Raymond Ernesto Colón, and Melinda Ackell for their dedication to turning my story into a book. And to the big kahuna herself, Erin Stein, hugs and kisses!

Michael, once again, you offered advice and guidance when I needed it. I admire your professionalism and honesty. Thank you.

A special thank-you to Sloane Leong and Rebecca Rialon Berry, PhD, for reviewing the book and sharing their thoughts with me.

Bob, Isabelle, and Walker, it's time for us to take another trip to Hawaii. Let's go!

GOFISH

SUZANNE SELFORS

What did you want to be when you grew up?
Anything to do with animals—a marine biologist, a naturalist, a zookeeper. I've always lived in a household filled with pets, which is probably why I often write about pets.

When did you realize you wanted to be a writer?
All during my childhood I wrote stories, but I never met a writer, never knew a writer, and because we never had any writers come to our school, I had no idea that I could actually write for a living. It took me a long time to work up the courage to try to write a novel and get it published. I was thirty-nine years old when I decided to give it a go!

What's your most embarrassing childhood memory?
When my underpants fell down to my ankles onstage during a kids' show called *Brakeman Bill*, in front of an audience. The elastic broke! Yep, that's a true story.

What's your favorite childhood memory?
Finding a stray dog at the library and taking her home. We named her Lulu, and she was with us for sixteen years.

What were your hobbies as a kid? What are your hobbies now?

As a kid I loved reading and acting in plays. I was in *The Wiz*, *Romeo and Juliet*, *Guys and Dolls*, and many other plays. I loved and still love dancing. I know how to fox-trot, Lindy Hop, waltz, salsa, and East Coast swing. I love bike riding and going boating on our boat, *The Flying Fish*.

Did you play sports as a kid?

I did not do sports as a kid because I'm not very competitive. Or aggressive. Plus, I don't like getting hurt. But I did a lot of dancing. I took ballet lessons for a long time.

What was your first job, and what was your "worst" job?

My first paid job, other than babysitting, was working at a deli counter at a Seattle deli.

My "worst" job was working at the Seattle Aquarium, where it was my duty to cut up buckets and buckets of squid, so the biologists could feed them to the seals. To this day I cannot eat squid.

What was your favorite book when you were a kid? Do you have a favorite book now?

My favorite book as a kid—and it's the same now—is any book by Roald Dahl. I am particularly fond of *Matilda*. I always wanted a teacher like Miss Honey.

What do you want readers to remember about your books?

My hope is that my books make people laugh. Truly that is the highest honor for me, when a reader tells me that my book is funny.

A strange and wonderful tale about
a girl and her magic farm.

Keep reading for an excerpt.

A SLIMY GIFT

Isabelle stood beneath a sky as gray as a pair of filthy socks. A horde of factory workers pushed past her, eager to get home to their suppers. Having eaten only half a cheese sandwich for lunch, Isabelle ached with hunger, but she needed to run an important errand before going back to the boardinghouse—a secret errand that couldn't wait.

"I can't come with you," said Gwen, who knew all about the secret errand because she was Isabelle's best friend. "I've got stupid dish duty tonight. See ya in the morning." She wiped her runny nose on her sleeve, then disappeared into the crowd.

"See ya," Isabelle called, zipping her yellow rain slicker all the way to her chin. Poor Gwen. Dish duty was never fun, and secret errands almost always were.

Clutching an empty water bottle, Isabelle hurried away from Runny Cove's Magnificently Supreme Umbrella Factory, where she had spent the entire day standing at a conveyor belt pressing labels onto boxes. Not the way most ten-year-olds would choose to spend the day, but Isabelle had no choice. Even though the work left her fingertips raw and made the soles of her feet ache, she never complained. Her boring job was the only reason she could buy half a cheese sandwich and a rain slicker. Without the umbrella factory, Isabelle would have nothing.

She followed the gravel road that led from the factory to the village of Runny Cove. Raindrops drummed against the sides of her plastic hood, a sound so commonplace that she barely even noticed. It rained every day in Runny Cove. It had for as long as Isabelle could remember. Sometimes the drops were as fat as thumbprints; sometimes they were almost invisible, forming a veil of mist. Sometimes they beat down so hard that they stung Isabelle's skin, while other times they dropped lazily from the sky like parachutists.

Because the clouds never parted in Runny Cove, the village was perpetually cast in a depressing shade of sludge—the same color as the gunky stuff that clogs up bathroom sinks. Never had Isabelle basked in the sun's warmth or strolled in the moon's light. Never had she known what it felt like to be completely dry. That was the cruel reality of Runny Cove, and that was why no one ever moved there. Isabelle couldn't blame them. Who would want to live in a gloomy place by the sea where it never stops raining, where everyone's skin is puckered and pale and covered in mold?

While most of the villagers chose to sit around and complain about the mud, acting all dreary about the rain as if it had seeped inside their skin and drowned their spirits, Isabelle's spirit refused to be extinguished, no matter how waterlogged it got. Ever heard the saying that if you've got lemons, you should make lemonade? Well, when you've got mud, you might as well make mud pies or mud forts. And that's exactly what Isabelle and her friends did. A lowly substance, mud, but with the right outlook it can offer up endless possibilities.

While the rest of the workers headed home into the village, Isabelle took a sharp turn off the road and started across the sand dunes. Dusk was falling, but like everyone else in Runny Cove, she was accustomed to dim light. Up and over the dunes she went, her mind fixated on her secret errand. She needed to get it done quickly so she could get back to Mama Lulu's Boardinghouse for supper.

Up and over, over and up she hurried, slowing only to cough. People who spend their days in damp undershirts and wet socks tend to get colds, which is the reason why most everyone in Runny Cove had a runny nose and a rib-splitting cough.

Though the crisp evening air tickled Isabelle's congested lungs, she kept her pace until she reached the driftwood forest. The logs lay in chaotic piles, some with sharp jutting branches, others with rotten patches that could break a leg. Isabelle had never seen a tightrope walker, but she resembled one as she held out her arms and tiptoed across, still clutching the empty bottle. She didn't feel a bit scared, since she had ventured to the beach many times by herself to explore or collect treasures. Excitement drove her onward. Her errand meant doing something different, something *interesting*, and she was one of those people who always managed to find bits of *interesting* in places where other people never looked.

As she crossed the driftwood, she sang one of her little songs at just the right tempo to match her careful steps. She sang loudly because there was no one around to yell, "Hey, kid! Stop making all that racket. Yer giving me a headache!"

Here's what she sang.

The Nowhere Song

Beyond the town, beyond the mill
beyond the river, beyond the hill
lies the land of Nowhere
and Nowhere lies there still,
for no one goes to Nowhere
and no one ever will.

It was a song she had made up about the mysterious place of her birth. At least that's what her Grandma Maxine had always told her whenever she had asked, "Where did I come from?"

"Nowhere."

"Is it far away?"

"I don't know. No one knows."

As much as Isabelle loved her grandmother, the lack of information was frustrating. A person has the right to know where she comes from. It's a perfectly reasonable request, not like asking for a new rain slicker when the old one has only a couple of holes. Gwen knew about her parents. She knew that her mother had died giving birth to her and that her father had died from a fever. It didn't make being an orphan any easier, but at least Gwen knew. Isabelle knew nothing.

"You've got to know *something*, Grandma. Think harder and you'll remember."

"It's no use asking me so many questions, Isabelle. All I know is that I found you one stormy morning. Nothing else. Just you, lying on the doorstep without a stitch of clothing, screaming so loud you drowned out the wind and rain. It seemed like you just appeared out of thin air."

"But I must have come from somewhere."

"As far as I can tell you came from nowhere, so please stop asking."

A girl who begins her life on a doorstep, without a note or clue of any kind, has a choice. She can believe that she was abandoned because no one wanted her, and she can feel like the most unimportant person in the world. Or she can believe, as Isabelle did, that because her origins were shrouded in mystery, that she must be an extra important person. A special person. A person like no other person.

For a secret birth is like a secret errand—sure to yield *something interesting*.

Isabelle reached the edge of the driftwood forest and, with a graceful jump, landed in the hard, wet sand that lay at the water's edge. The cove formed a crescent as gray as the sky above, littered with the hulls of long-abandoned fishing boats. Creosote-covered pilings poked out of the water, all that remained of the docks that used to line the beach.

Grandma Maxine had told her that the boats used to go out each morning and return each evening, overflowing with fish. But no one fished the cove anymore, not since the fish had gone away.

Isabelle twisted the cap off the empty bottle and waded into the water. As she submerged the bottle, air bubbles rose to the surface, bobbing between raindrops. When the bottle had filled, she recapped it and shoved it into her pocket. Her stomach growled. Mama Lulu would be serving supper soon. Her errand completed, Isabelle was about to start home when a roar rose above the rain's drumming—a roar far too loud to be her stomach.

Something moved in the water where the cove met the sea. Isabelle pushed off her hood, trying to get a better view. The something was much bigger than she, and swimming toward her. She took a few steps backward as it moved closer. She'd never seen anything like it. Could it be dangerous?

She ran up the beach to the edge of the driftwood forest, where she watched, openmouthed, as the large thing emerged from the shallow water. It was a creature of some sort, and it pulled its enormous, blubbery body onto the sand with a pair of front flippers. The strangest nose hung from the middle of its face, swaying back and forth as it heaved itself up the beach. She couldn't see its mouth but imagined a vast row of sharp teeth. If it didn't eat her alive, surely it would flatten her like a skipping stone. Terrified, she scrambled up some driftwood but lost her footing and fell back onto the sand.

ROARRRRR!

With a burst of speed, the creature galloped up the beach and parked itself at Isabelle's feet. She froze, remembering that the fishermen who had fished the cove long ago had believed in sea monsters that sank ships and ate the crew.

Hot breath seared Isabelle's face. Large black eyes, surrounded by folds of skin, stared down at her. "Please don't eat me," she begged, squeezing her eyes shut. Being eaten alive wasn't something she wanted to watch. She waited for deep, horrible pain. But a few moments passed and nothing happened. Slowly, she opened her eyes.

Still staring, the monster cocked its head. Raindrops rolled down skin that looked like rubber. It sniffed her hair with its long nose.

"Please, please don't eat me," Isabelle whimpered, scooting back against the driftwood pile.

It raised its nose and opened its mouth. Isabelle squealed and pushed against the wood, hoping to find a spot where she could disappear. But she was trapped. She was going to die without having said good-bye to her grandmother or to Gwen. She was about to become supper! "Help!" she cried, though she knew no one would hear.

The sea monster took a great breath, then sneezed. The force of the sneeze knocked Isabelle sideways. Slime shot out the end of the dangly nose and landed in Isabelle's short hair. Disgusting! "Cover your nose when you sneeze," Grandma Maxine always said. But Isabelle wasn't about to correct a sea monster's manners.

"You can sneeze on me as much as you'd like. Just please don't eat me." She pulled on her hood as the creature took another breath and sneezed again. This time, something else flew out of its nose and landed with a *thunk* in Isabelle's lap.

The creature tapped its flipper impatiently and grunted, as if waiting for something. The rain beat harder. Isabelle peered out from under her hood. She didn't know what to do. What could it possibly be waiting for?

"Bless you?" she whispered. It continued to stare. "Bless you two times?"

The nose reached forward and pointed at Isabelle's lap. She grimaced, expecting to find a giant booger, but found, instead, a slime-covered red apple.

A real, honest-to-goodness apple.

No apples grew in Runny Cove or in the wetlands that lay outside the village. Apples occasionally showed up at the factory's grocery store, but only Mr. Supreme's assistants could afford to buy them. Isabelle had never tasted one. She had never even held one. She picked it up. It would cost an entire day's wages to buy one half the size. The sea monster grunted again. "Oh, I'm sorry. Here." She held it out. Should she stick the apple back up its nose?

To her amazement, the sea monster shook its head. "Don't you want it back?"

It shook its head again. Then, with a roar that vibrated Isabelle's teeth, it turned and made its way back to the water. It hadn't eaten her. It hadn't flattened her. It had only sneezed on her. "THANK YOU!" she yelled, waving the apple.

It turned and nodded, its nose bouncing up and down.

Then it swam out of sight. "Wow," Isabelle whispered.

Other than being left on a doorstep, this was the most

special thing that had ever happened to Isabelle. Even though slime coated her hair and face, and even though she had been scared half to death, she smiled. Gwen would never believe it. Wouldn't Grandma Maxine be surprised? No one in Runny Cove had ever met a sea monster. No factory worker had ever been given an apple.

She checked to make certain that the water bottle was safe in one pocket and tucked the apple securely into another pocket. Then she climbed onto the driftwood pile and ran back toward the village, feeling extra, extra special.

MAMA LULU

Water sloshed against Isabelle's boots as she ran down Boggy Lane. The cobblestone lane dipped into the lowest part of the village, so it was always flooded. As her hood bounced at the back of her neck, rain washed all the sea monster snot from her face and hair.

Lights glowed from the kitchen windows of the old, battered boardinghouses lining the lane. Greasy odors wafted out through cracks in the house boards, aggravating Isabelle's hunger pains. She wondered if the apple would be edible after traveling inside a nose. She plucked it from her pocket and held it beneath a gushing rainspout. It was bigger and shinier than any apple in the factory store, and she could have eaten it right there, but then she'd have no proof of her adventure. Besides, something that wonderful had to be shared.

Boggy Lane took a sharp turn, then ended at Mama Lulu's Boardinghouse. A vacancy sign swayed from the rafter, pushed by the wind and rain. No one had moved to Runny Cove for as long as Isabelle could remember, but Mama Lulu still insisted on advertising. Isabelle ran up the stone steps and threw herself against the front door, which swelled in particularly nasty weather and needed a good shove to open.

"Yer late!" Mama Lulu hollered from the kitchen.

"Sorry," Isabelle called, closing the door. Of course, she didn't regret her trip to the beach, not one bit.

The entryway felt chilly, as usual. The sour smell of boiled cabbage hung in the air. A frying pan sat on the floor, collecting water that dripped from a seam in the wall. Isabelle slipped off her boots and placed them neatly at the end of the boot shelf. She removed her rain slicker and hung it on the rack next to the other slickers. She decided to leave the filled water bottle in her slicker's pocket and get it after supper. The apple, however, was another matter. Mama Lulu liked to snoop through pockets, and while she'd have no interest in a bottle filled with seawater, if she found the apple she'd claim it for herself.

"This house belongs to me," she often reminded her tenants. "So everything in it belongs to me, too."

Isabelle tucked the apple into the waistband of her canvas pants. Her flannel shirt, a hand-me-down from another tenant, was four sizes too large, so it did a good job concealing the lump.

"Did ya check fer slugs?" Mama Lulu bellowed. The boardinghouse's proprietor despised slugs. In fact, she hated them so much that the mere act of seeing one drove her into a tizzy. Unfortunately, Runny Cove possessed more slugs than any other place on earth. The little gastropods bred in every damp nook and cranny the village had to offer. They gobbled up anything the villagers tried to grow, leaving trails of slime in their wake. If a slug wanted to move across town, it would attach itself to a boot or pant leg when a villager walked down the street, or drop from an eave to hitchhike on a hood or in someone's hair. Mama Lulu had decreed that anyone who brought a slug into her house would lose blanket privileges for a month. "Did ya check?"

In all her excitement, Isabelle had forgotten to check. "Yes, I checked," she lied, quickly sliding her hands through her hair.